*"Life takes you to unexpected places.
Love brings you home."*

—MELISSA McCLONE

LOVE'S A MYSTERY

in

TOMBSTONE AZ

BETHANY JOHN
& GAIL KIRKPATRICK

Love's a Mystery is a trademark of Guideposts.

Published by Guideposts
100 Reserve Road, Suite E200
Danbury, CT 06810
Guideposts.org

Cover and interior design by Müllerhaus.
Cover illustration by Dan Burr at Illustration Online LLC.
Typeset by Aptara, Inc.

ISBN 978-1-961441-46-0 (hardcover)
ISBN 978-1-961441-47-7 (softcover)
ISBN 978-1-959633-29-7 (epub)

Printed and bound in the United States of America

REBUILDING LOVE

by

BETHANY JOHN

"An exceptional future can only be built on the transformation of the mess I've made out of my past, not the elimination of that mess."

—Craig D. Lounsbrough

CHAPTER ONE

In their hearts humans plan their course, but the
Lord establishes their steps.
—Proverbs 16:9

Tombstone, Arizona
1976

"You summoned me, Counselor?"

Wyatt Clark looked over his shoulder to see his best friend's kid sister, Wilhelmina—Billie—Keenan walk through the door of the Rusty Spur, his family's Old West-themed restaurant that had recently shut its doors.

"Summoned?" he questioned as he took a good look at her. He shouldn't think of her as a kid anymore. She was twenty-seven now. All physical traces of the girl she had been faded away. Her braces were gone. Her frizzy red hair had magically transformed into shiny auburn curls. She wasn't dressed like she was as a child. Long gone were the smock dresses her grandmother had sewn by hand. They had been replaced by a fashionable pair of bell-bottom jeans and the kind of blouse his sister called a "peasant top." He could see that her time away from Tombstone had altered her a little. There was a sophistication to her, a confidence that he hadn't known her to have when they were growing up. If she weren't his best friend's annoying little sister, Wyatt might even call her beautiful.

"I didn't 'summon' you," he said. "I simply called and asked if you would meet me here."

"You didn't call me. You called my brother, who called my mother, who told me to get myself to the Rusty Spur because you wanted to see me. If that's not summoning, I don't know what is."

"I didn't have your phone number," he said. He could have asked Randy for it, but he felt weird doing that.

"I'll give it to you today. Although it might change soon," she said proudly. "I'm considering a job in New York. One of the biggest banks in the world offered me a position."

"New York?" He was alarmed to hear that. That would take her all the way to the other side of the country. They were both born and raised in Tombstone. New York would be another world for her. "Are you sure you want to move there? You've seen the news. It's not exactly a safe city. It's also thousands of miles away. What if something happened? It would be hard for anyone to get to you."

Billie narrowed her eyes at him, annoyance creeping across her face. "How about a congratulations? This a big deal. They don't take just anyone, you know."

"I'm happy that you were offered such a great opportunity. You deserve it. I was just in New York for a work trip. It was an experience. Stay out of Times Square." He couldn't see her there. He couldn't picture her so far away.

He didn't want her so far away.

"Aren't you being hypocritical? You took a job in San Francisco. It's not the safest city in the world either. There's crime everywhere. How can you give me grief for it?"

"I'm not giving you grief. I'm just concerned. You also can't compare us. I'm a six-foot-one 200-pound former football player. People tend not to mess with me, and if they did, I can handle myself."

"And I'm a five-foot-seven former math club champ who grew up with a six-foot-three brother and his annoying six-foot-one best friend who used to put me in headlocks every chance he got. I'm not fragile."

"I wasn't trying to hurt you then," he blurted out, feeling exasperated by how she couldn't see the difference. "I care about you. I would worry about you by yourself in New York." He hadn't meant to say it, but he had, and it was the truth.

The annoyance melted from her face, and she blinked at him for a long moment. "I said I've been offered a job. I didn't say I'd taken it. I've also interviewed for a job in Phoenix. It's a state job, not as fast-paced, good benefits. I'm waiting to hear back."

Phoenix was still a good three hours away, but it wasn't New York.

"You'll get it." He motioned to a table, inviting her to sit. "You're in demand. You're the smartest person I know when it comes to numbers, and now you have an MBA to go with your accounting degree. There's no reason not to hire you."

"Why are you being so nice to me?" She looked around the empty restaurant suspiciously. "And why are we here? I thought your uncle put the place on the market."

He frowned. "What do you mean, why am I being so nice to you? I'm always nice to you."

"Oh, forgive me, I must have been imagining all the headlocks, hairpulling, and general teasing when we were kids."

"*Kids*. I'm thirty now. When's the last time I put you in a headlock? In fact, when was the last time I saw you? I've haven't been home in two years, and the last time I was, you were away at school."

"Has it been that long?" She looked thoughtful for a moment. "I guess it has. You wrote to me, so maybe that's why it doesn't feel as long."

He had sent her letters. On her birthday and on holidays and whenever he thought about her. Once in a while he'd included little gifts. Sometimes he sent her chocolate, other times he sent her a book he thought she would like. He got her parents and Randy gifts as well, but she was the only one he wrote to.

He clearly remembered the last time he did. It was her birthday, a little over a month ago, when he decided to leave his job and come back home. He sent her a pair of earrings, which were in her ears right now. It made him feel good to see them there.

"I'm home for good, Billie. I've quit my job."

Her mouth dropped open, a gasp escaping. "You're home for good? There can't be many corporate law jobs here in Tombstone. Are you going to switch specialties? I guess if you open a small practice in town, you might be able to generate enough business. People always seem to need lawyers."

"I don't want to be a lawyer any longer. I came home to reopen the restaurant."

"What? You're going to reopen this place? But your uncle wants to retire, spend his golden years on a beach somewhere."

"He can do that. And I can do this. I've got some ideas on how to make it bigger and better than before. There's a new resort opening in town, and there's going to be a ton of tourists looking for a good place to eat. This can be that place."

"But you really want to run a restaurant? You haven't worked in here since you went to law school. There's so much that goes into it. Don't you know that 80 percent of restaurants fail within their first five years? It's a very risky business to get into."

Always practical. Always armed with facts. It was one of the reasons he needed her.

"But this restaurant isn't new. My great-grandfather started it over sixty years ago. People came then. They'll come again."

She looked at him and then around the empty restaurant. All that was left were some tables and chairs that had seen better days. Otherwise, his uncle had cleaned the place out completely. Tossed everything. Wyatt didn't even get a chance to save the old photograph of Wyatt Earp that used to hang on the wall over the register.

The emptiness of it all made him sad. Some of his best memories were here.

"I can't sit by and allow this place to close. It's where we both earned our first paycheck. It's where I learned how to work hard. I've done every job you could possibly do here, down to cleaning the toilets. I know I can run this place. Besides, legally, it's half mine. My father's share passed to me when he died. I can't let go of it."

She reached across the table and set her hand over his. Only she knew how hard the loss of his father was on him. It wasn't something he could share with Randy. He even had a hard time talking about it with his mother, but for some reason, he could talk to Billie. It was why he had asked to see her. He needed her to start this journey with him.

Billie looked at Wyatt for a long moment. He was no longer the silly boy who used to be at her house so often that she almost thought he lived there. He had matured. He had always been handsome. Every girl in her grade had a crush on him, but the boy with the good looks had morphed into a man who was ruggedly handsome. It was so odd to her that he had chosen to become a corporate lawyer when he looked more like a cowboy. He had dark hair, dark eyes, and broad shoulders. It was hard to imagine him stuck behind a desk all day, wearing a suit that he must have felt like he was suffocating in.

He had never told her he was unhappy with his chosen career. But she suspected he was by the tone of his last few letters.

He was more than her brother's friend. He was like family, and even though they hadn't seen much of each other these past five years, she knew him better than she had ever known anyone else.

"What do you need from me? My blessing? You have it. If you've got your heart set on doing something, how could I not support it?"

"I do need your blessing. No one else in my family is on board with this."

"Really? Not even your mother?"

"My mother loves to tell people that her son is an attorney living in California. Owning an Old West-themed restaurant wasn't in her plans for me."

"I'll support you. What does Randy think of it?"

"He doesn't know. I haven't told him yet."

"Why not?" She was surprised that Wyatt had decided to tell her first. "I'm sure he'll support you too."

"I didn't want to tell him until I had spoken to you first."

"But why?" She frowned in confusion.

"I need your help."

"Me?"

"Yes, you. Why do you seem so shocked? You're the most organized person I know. You have degrees in accounting and business, and you're the only one who's honest enough to tell me if I'm being ridiculous. Please, don't say no. I need you."

I need you.

His words, the way he said them, struck her right in the chest. He had never asked her for anything.

"How long would I be helping you?"

His eyes widened with excitement, and a boyish grin crept over his face. "You'll do it?"

"Answer my question first."

"Just the summer. Until we open. And I'll pay you a fair rate."

"Of course you will. Do you think I work for free?"

He stood up, grabbed her hand, and yanked her out of her chair and into a hug. "Thank you, Billie," he said in her ear. She shut her eyes and leaned into him for a moment. But it was only a moment, because he twisted her around and put her in a headlock.

"You're never too old for this."

"Let go of me, you big oaf!"

He did, still grinning at her. "Got to keep you on your toes." He surprised her again by smoothing her hair. It was a gentle touch that jolted her much more than the headlock. "Can't let you leave with your hair standing up all over your head."

She lightly slapped his hand away. "Don't touch me, goof."

"I promise I'll try to refrain from doing that while we're working together. Can you meet me back here around six? I want to show you the plans I drew up and see what you think."

"That's dinnertime."

"Don't worry. I'll feed you."

He took a key out of his pocket and handed it to her. "This is for you. It opens both the front and the back doors so you can come and go whenever you need to."

"You have a key for me already?" she asked as she stared down at it.

"Yeah. I picked up the copy this morning."

"How were you so sure I would say yes?"

"I had faith." He grinned at her again and set off toward the door. "Lock up when you go. I need to take care of some things before tonight."

He left her alone in the restaurant. He seemed deliriously happy, but Billie wondered if she was getting in over her head.

⁓❀ CHAPTER TWO ❀⁓

"Have I not commanded you? Be strong and courageous.
Do not be afraid; do not be discouraged, for the LORD *your*
God will be with you wherever you go."
—*Joshua 1:9*

"Are you hungry?" Wyatt's uncle asked him for the third time. "I know you said no already, but when's the last time you had something to eat? You can't live on coffee all day. At least have a piece of cake. Your aunt made it."

Wyatt sighed, trying not to feel frustrated with his uncle, but he was failing. He'd been at his uncle's house for over an hour already, and he hadn't gotten anywhere. "If I have a piece of cake, will you sit down and talk to me about the restaurant?"

"What's there to talk about? I didn't want to run it anymore, so I closed it. End of story."

"Yes, but I want to run it now, so it's not the end of the story. It's the beginning of a new one. I want to see the financial records. Your food costs. Your suppliers. How much were your payroll expenses? How were your profits from month to month, and year to year?"

"We did okay. I put your half of the money in an account for you. It's a decent amount."

"Yes, but where are the records?"

Uncle John waved him off again and turned to cut the cake. "Your father was the one who was good at taking care of that stuff. I'm not so uptight about it. I didn't keep track of every little thing."

"What about taxes? If there's one thing the government doesn't let slide, it's taxes."

"I paid the taxes. Too much, if you ask me. That I could probably dig up for you. Might take me a few days to find it though."

"A few days?"

"We moved everything out of the restaurant. Some things are in the garage. Some things are at your mother's house. Other things are at the town dump. I'll see what I can find. We can always request another copy from the government. That could take a while." He looked back at him. "You want milk? I could put a few ice cubes in it for you. You used to like that when you were a kid."

"Yeah. Sure." Wyatt really wanted to take his uncle to task for being so careless with important documents, but he chose to stay quiet instead. Uncle John was a stubborn old goat at times, and if Wyatt pushed any harder, he would shut down.

"Look at this cake. Beautiful, isn't it?" He set it on the table with a tall glass of milk. This was a ritual they'd had when Wyatt was a kid. He would go directly to the Rusty Spur right after school. He had his own seat at the counter, where his uncle would bring him whatever dessert they were serving that day and a big glass of milk with ice. He wasn't exactly sure when he'd stopped going. Probably when he was in high school, and sports and other teenage things took over his time and attention.

He dug his fork into the cake. It was chocolate with a thick, decadent buttercream frosting. He had dined in some of the finest restaurants in California. Had desserts made by world-renowned pastry chefs. But nothing was better than this rustic-looking cake that Aunt Sarah made in Tombstone, Arizona.

"It's mighty good, isn't it?"

"It's amazing," he admitted. "I've missed this."

"If you missed your aunt's baking, we could have mailed you some cookies or something. You didn't have to quit your job, *your very good job,* and move home to get it."

"You would have mailed me cookies? Hmm, I didn't think of that. Maybe I can call and get my job back."

"Ha ha, Mr. Funny. It's hard for us to wrap our heads around you quitting your job."

"I didn't like my job, and I wanted to come home. Why is that hard to understand?"

"If everyone quit their job just because they didn't like it, no one would work. You don't work because you like it. You work for money, and you were making a lot of it."

His uncle was right. He had made a lot of money. But it brought him little else. No joy. No peace. No fulfillment.

"Speaking of money, why haven't you cashed my check to buy you out of the business?"

"Because any day now I'm expecting you to come to your senses so I can put the restaurant on the market and we both can make some money."

"Is the amount I offered not enough? Is that what the problem is? I can pay more."

"No. It's more than enough. But you know the new resort that's opening in town? The owner was interested in buying the building and having the restaurant be an event space for them. So people could feel like they were leaving the resort but the resort would still get their money. I didn't think it was a bad idea."

"It's not a bad idea. But it's not the idea I have. I want to breathe some new life into the Rusty Spur. Make it fun again. This is Tombstone. People love the nostalgia. We could give them a real Wild West experience and good food, which a lot of tourist places are lacking."

"*We* can't do anything." He grabbed another fork from the drawer, stuck it into the cake, and took a bite. "I'm retired, remember? I want out of the restaurant business. I told the resort owner that maybe he should open a disco and forget about serving food altogether. Give the young people somewhere to dance. Not everyone likes country and western music."

"A disco?"

"I would like to go to one. Just to see what it looks like. I was hoping you would take me to one when I visited you in San Francisco, but you moved back here, and now you want to reopen the restaurant. Looks like I'll never get to go to one now." He took another bite of his cake.

Wyatt sighed. It looked like he would have to do this without his uncle's help.

Billie walked into the Rusty Spur two minutes before six. Unlike this morning, Wyatt wasn't waiting for her in the front. It was almost eerie being in the restaurant when it was empty. It wasn't just the lack of patrons. It was the lack of everything. There used to be a life-size statue of a horse at the front door. Everyone in town probably had a picture of themselves in front of that horse. It was like a landmark, a rite of passage almost. But now it was gone, and just a few tables and chairs remained. None of the kooky fun decor was left. It was a completely blank slate, ready for the next owner to make it into whatever they wanted it to be.

And that next owner was Wyatt. She hadn't been surprised when his uncle John decided to close the place. His heart wasn't in it anymore. Over the years, little things started to slip away. There was no more line dancing on Thursday nights. They stopped serving brunch on Sundays for the after-church crowd. There wasn't a push to cater to tourists. Billie understood that things had to change, but she had been sad to hear that Mr. Clark shut the place down. So much of her life was spent here. She had always expected to be able to come home and come here.

"Wyatt?" she called as she made her way through the dining room.

"I'm up here," he called back. There was a little apartment hidden in the rear of the restaurant. It had been occupied by the old cook, Shelby, when they were kids, but in the past few years, it was used for storage. Billie followed Wyatt's voice up the stairs, expecting the apartment to be full of clutter. But it too had been cleared out except for a few pieces of furniture: a small table, a couch that must have been there since the early '50s, and an equally old television.

Wyatt was in the tiny kitchen, standing over the stove. It was then that a savory smell hit her nose, and her stomach began to growl.

"It's really weird to see you cooking." She sat down and watched him for a moment. He seemed like he knew what he was doing. It wasn't what she had expected from him. The last time she had seen him was when she and Randy went to visit him in San Francisco. He lived in a luxurious apartment and took them to eat in expensive restaurants. They even went to a show. It was a different world than the three kids from Tombstone had known. Billie had to admit she was impressed with the life Wyatt had built for himself, but she knew it wasn't the kind of life she wanted to live.

"What do you mean? I worked in the kitchen here when we were teenagers."

"I guess. But you mostly waited tables. I remember there was always a group of cheerleaders who just had to sit in your section back then."

"I gave excellent service. Of course they wanted to sit in my section."

"I thought this apartment would be full of stuff, but your uncle really got rid of everything, didn't he?"

"Everything. Even the records. I had hoped there would be something here, but there isn't."

"Did you know he was going to close it?"

"Not a clue." He plated the food and set it on the table in front of her. "My special meat loaf, mashed potatoes, and broccoli. I put a little cheese on the broccoli for you because I know you like that."

It looked delicious and smelled even better. "This looks good. What did you put in it? Am I going to find a worm in the meat loaf? Did you put sugar instead of salt in the potatoes?"

"We only tried to make you eat a worm once, and I was ten years old then. I don't mess with food. Go on, try it. Besides, it would be pretty dumb of me to sabotage the food of the person I need to help me."

She took a bite of the meat loaf and had to close her eyes for a moment as the rich gravy, perfectly cooked onion, and juicy beef flooded her taste buds.

"Is it good?"

She opened her eyes and looked at him. He stared at her intently, as if he waited for her approval. "It's incredible. Where did you learn to cook like this?"

"I've had to feed myself for the past few years. I've picked up a thing or two."

"I've also had to feed myself for the past few years. I haven't picked up anything like this."

"You think this is something that could go on the menu?" He took a seat across from her and started on his own meal.

"Yes. It's delicious. Have you been thinking about the menu already?"

"I've been thinking about everything, but I think the menu is probably the most important. There are a dozen cowboy-themed restaurants here. We have to stick out."

"Tell me what you're thinking."

"I want it to be all-American hearty food with a little sophistication to it. More than just your basic steaks and chicken. I want people to come to the Rusty Spur to celebrate special occasions. I want people to make a special trip to see us."

He got up from his chair and took a thick folder off the counter. "I've been keeping my ideas in here. I was hoping you could look them over and tell me which ones are feasible and which ones you think are pipe dreams."

She started to take the folder from him, but he held it away from her. "Eat first. I don't want your food to get cold."

He was excited about this. She could hear it in his voice. "Have you shown the plans to your uncle?"

"No. I would if he was at all interested in seeing them, but when I spoke to him today, he didn't want to hear about any of it. He was checked out. He's serious about not being involved at all. I guess I have to respect that."

"On the one hand, I understand. When my mother retired from teaching, she didn't want a child within a ten-mile radius of her. She's softened up a little since. Maybe your uncle is just burned out. You haven't lived here full-time since you were eighteen. He's been running that restaurant alone with no family support for the past twelve years. Let him unwind. I'm sure he'll take an interest once he understands that this is more than just a hobby for you."

He nodded. "I had a client who gifted me some weeks at his resorts. I want to send Uncle John and Aunt Sarah to Hawaii, but I think he's too proud to accept a trip from me. He won't even cash the check I gave him to buy him out of the restaurant."

"Just mention it casually to him and see if he's interested. If you make it seem like it's his idea, he might go for it." They continued to eat for a few minutes in silence. It wasn't because Billie didn't have anything to say. She did. In fact, she had a dozen questions, but one was on her mind more than anything else. "Wyatt?"

"What's up? Do you want more? I have plenty left."

She smiled at him. "You sound like my mother." She shook her head. "I know you're really excited about reopening the restaurant, but will you stay excited? Once it's open and it's just about managing the day-to-day things, are you going to be passionate about it? Or will you get bored and move on to the next thing? I'll help you either way, but be honest with me and yourself. Is this restaurant something you can see yourself running in the long term?"

Billie's question took him off guard. Their entire relationship had always been built around teasing each other. He was seeing a different side of her today.

Over the past few years, they had only communicated through letters. But now he could look at her, hear her voice, take all of her in. Today he was actually seeing her. Had her eyes always been that big? Had they always had that little bit of green sprinkled in them? Had her skin always looked so soft and smooth?

He shook those thoughts out of his head. They distracted him from the conversation at hand.

It was a good question, one he had asked himself just before he packed his belongings and booked a one-way ticket home. She deserved more than a glib response, and he thought about how to answer her question for a long moment. He opened his mouth to speak, and in that moment the lights went out.

"What in the world?" he heard Billie say. He could no longer see her. It was pitch-black in the room.

"I wonder if there's some sort of blackout." He got up from the table and slowly made his way to the window, where he could see faint light. They were located at the end of the street, a little distance from where most of the other businesses were. There was nothing ahead of him except the moonlight and the Arizona desert, but off to the right, Wyatt could see lights from the resort that was still under construction. It was the biggest thing this town had ever seen. "No blackout. Everyone else appears to have lights. I think it's just us."

"Do you have a flashlight in here?" Billie asked him.

"No, but there are candles in one of the kitchen drawers. I saw them today. We should probably light a couple."

He started to head toward the kitchen, but his progress was stopped when he ran into something.

"Ouch!" Billie yelped. "You bozo. That was my head you ran into."

"What are you doing moving around?"

"I was going to get the candles."

"I was also going to get the candles. We both can't be wandering around in the dark. Sit down before one of us ends up with a concussion."

"I won't sit down. It's mostly because I can't see the chair and don't want to end up on the floor, but I don't like you telling me what to do either."

"Just stay still then." He made his way to the kitchen and felt around in one of the drawers until he touched the smooth wax of the candles. He pulled two out along with a box of matches. Soon he was able to light one of the candles, and Billie once again appeared in his sight. Her eyes were wide with worry mixed with a little fear. He wanted to comfort her, but he didn't know what was going on or what exactly to do about it. "Come take this candle. I'm going to light another one. Then I'm going to go downstairs and check the circuit breaker."

She took the candle from him. "You are not leaving me alone up here. Are you out of your mind?"

"Fine. Then come with me," he said while lighting the other candle. He looked back at her. "I didn't think you were afraid of the dark."

"I'm not!"

"Then why don't you want to stay here while I go downstairs?"

"What if something happens to you while you're down there? You could fall or be attacked by a wild animal. My going with you is for *your* protection."

He grinned at her for a moment and then shook his head. "Of course. Why didn't I think of that?" He made his way to the door. "Let's go see what's up."

She followed closely behind him as they walked down the stairs. Their two candles were barely enough light to illuminate the space inches before their faces. Once they reached the ground floor, Wyatt immediately noticed that the kitchen door was wide open.

"You didn't come through the back door, did you?" he asked.

"No. I came in through the front door. But I had to walk through the kitchen to find you, and that door was definitely closed."

Wyatt began to feel uneasy.

"Do you think someone tried to break in?" Her question could have come from his own mind.

"It's possible, but there's nothing in here to take." He took a step toward the door to see if anyone was out there, but he felt the warmth of Billie's presence on his back. "Is there anything I can say to get you to stay here while I go check the door?"

"Nope. Where you go I go."

He sighed. They walked to the wide-open door that led to the back of the restaurant. He saw no one, just some empty dumpsters. He checked the door to see if there was any sign of tampering or a break-in. There was none.

"I would say the wind did it, but there's not even a breeze," Billie said softly.

"No." He didn't want to say it aloud, but he had a feeling someone had opened that door.

He walked back inside and directly to the breaker box. Sure enough, the main power switch was flipped to the off position.

"You think someone shut off the power?" she asked.

"I don't want to say that, but I can't think of any other explanation." He flipped the switch, and immediately the light hit them. He took the candle from her and blew both out before tossing them on the counter. "But why would someone do that?"

"Maybe they thought the place was abandoned. It's not out of the ordinary for people to break into places they think are empty. Maybe they heard us upstairs and got scared away."

"That's possible."

"Do a lot of people know about your plan to reopen the restaurant?"

"Just you and my family. I haven't reached out to anyone yet to start any work."

"No one knows you're here tonight?"

"My mother knows. I told her I was going to live here instead of with her while I got things off the ground. She wasn't thrilled about it."

"Well, mystery solved. Your mother did it."

"Yes. I can just see my sixty-five-year-old mother slinking around in the dark, shutting off power just to mess with me."

She shrugged. "Don't ever underestimate an annoyed mother. They'll surprise you every time."

"I'm going to get a lock for this panel just to be safe. I also have to call someone over to check all the appliances."

"It would make sense to know what we're starting with so we can make a reasonable plan. How much is your budget?"

"I'm putting everything my uncle socked away for me when my father died into the restaurant. It's around twenty-five thousand."

"That's a hunk of cash. I guess we should get back to work."

He was surprised by her response. "You want to go back to work after everything that just went down?"

"Yes, and I would prefer to do it over ice cream. Go get your car keys. We're going to the diner."

∿ CHAPTER THREE ∿

For the Spirit God gave us does not make us timid,
but gives us power, love and self-discipline.
—2 Timothy 1:7

Wyatt knocked on his best friend's door the next morning. Randy's wife, Flora, opened the door and greeted him with a warm smile.

"Wyatt!" Flora kissed his cheek and gave him a warm hug. "I heard you were in town. We were away visiting my family when you arrived. Come in. I'll feed you breakfast."

"Flora, please don't go out of your way. I just wanted to say hello to Randy."

"He's getting dressed, and I have to make breakfast anyway. It's no bother."

Randy had been married to Flora a little over five years now, and Wyatt thought it was one of the best things he had ever done. Randy was a giant man with a hard exterior. Flora was his opposite in every way. Sweet. Smiley. Gentle. They were both teachers at the local high school when they met. Flora taught Spanish. Randy was the physical-education teacher and the football coach.

"You wouldn't happen to have any of that sweet bread, would you? I've been thinking about it since the last time I saw you."

"Of course. You want coffee or my special hot chocolate with it?"

"Hot chocolate sounds good. Thank you."

She smiled brightly at him and led him to the kitchen. He took a seat at the table. He liked their home. It wasn't like anything he had seen in San Francisco. The house had a cozy feel even though they were in the middle of a desert. The kitchen was decorated in warm reds, browns, and the harvest gold of the appliances. There was art everywhere: little statues, paintings, extravagantly patterned rugs. He'd never expected Randy to stay in Tombstone. If he hadn't gotten hurt the end of his senior year, Randy would have likely played football professionally.

"You always look beautiful, but you look especially gorgeous today, Flora."

She waved her hand in dismissal. "You're such a charmer."

"Who's a charmer?" He heard Randy's deep voice come from the other room. "Why do I hear a man's voice in my house?"

"I've come to steal your wife," Wyatt replied as Randy walked into the kitchen.

"Hey, Wyatt!" He gave him a friendly slap on the back before he walked over to his wife and wrapped his massive arm around her. "Did you tell him the news?" he asked her.

"No. I thought you wanted to tell him."

Randy's hand slid to his wife's stomach, and love filled his face.

"You're having a baby!" Wyatt got up and hugged Flora and then his friend. "Congratulations! You're going to be great parents."

"Thank you," Flora said. "We're excited. You'll have to come back when the baby is born."

"I don't have to come back, because I'm not leaving. I live here now."

"You do?" Randy's eyes went wide. "You left your job. Did something happen?"

"My uncle closed the restaurant is what happened. I'm going to reopen it."

"Wow." He sat down at the table. "I was surprised when he closed it without telling anyone. But I'm more surprised you would give up your career to run a restaurant. You had such a nice life."

"I made money. I wouldn't say I made a life there. Now I can be here and see your kid grow up. I just saw Billie yesterday. She didn't mention anything about a baby."

"We haven't told anyone yet," Flora said. "You're the first to know. I'm a little cautious. I wanted to wait till I was sure everything was okay. We're going to tell Randy's parents today." She turned away from them and started preparing breakfast.

"What did you want Billie for anyway?" Randy asked.

"I hired her for the summer to help with opening the restaurant. She's going to handle all the finances."

Randy nodded. "She told you she got that job offer in New York?"

"She did." He frowned. "Why are you letting her even consider moving to the other side of the country?"

"Have you met my sister? There isn't a thing I can do to stop her. She's not a kid anymore."

He was right about that. The longer he spent with her, the more he understood that. "I don't like the idea of her in New York. Anything could happen."

"Anything could happen anywhere. I have to trust that Billie knows what's best for her. Besides, she's stubborn. If I say anything, she'll move there just to spite me."

"She told me she was up for a job in Phoenix too. It's still three hours away, but it's closer."

"There's not a lot of opportunity for someone like Billie in Tombstone. What could she do here? Work for one of the hotels or in a gift shop? If it wasn't good enough for you, why would it be good enough for her?"

"I never said Tombstone wasn't good enough for me."

"You didn't have to say it. Everyone knew you would leave here as soon as you could. You got your opportunity to see the world. Now it's her turn."

"I can understand Wyatt being a little overprotective," Flora interjected. "He's probably just worried about her. Tell me more about your plans for the restaurant," she said, changing the subject, probably sensing that things were getting slightly heated. "I'm excited that you're going to reopen it. I know you all practically grew up in there."

"I'm just in the beginning stages. It's been closed down for a few months. I need to see what works and what needs replacing, and then I can go from there."

"That seems like a logical first step," Randy said. "Let me know how I can help. I was sad to see it go."

"If you know of any kids looking for work, send them my way. I'm hoping to open by Labor Day. I have a feeling I can use all the help I can get."

He chatted with them for a few more minutes before he left. There were too many thoughts crashing around in his head. The list of things he needed to do was growing longer and longer.

Billie was sitting at the counter when she heard the front door to the restaurant open and saw Wyatt walk in. Immediately she could tell that something was wrong. She wondered if last night still weighed on his mind. It had to be. It weighed on hers. Someone had to have come in last night. They shut off the power. There could be no pure motives for that, and she couldn't help but worry for his safety. He'd come back here last night after they left the diner. She knew he was a big man who could take care of himself, but that didn't soothe her anxiety about him being here alone overnight.

"Hey. I didn't think you would arrive so early," he said.

"This is my job. I'll be here by nine every day. I looked over your plans last night and came up with a categorized preliminary budget. Your biggest preopening expense looks like it's going to be redecorating. Especially if you want to section off the back area for private parties." She handed him the report she had prepared. "I also made a list of all the people who still worked here when it closed. Maybe you can entice some of them to return. It would be easier than having to train an all-new staff."

"Wilhelmina, you are incredible."

"You know I hate to be called that!"

"It's your name," he retorted. "Also, when you impress me this much, calling you Billie doesn't seem sufficient. How do you know who was working here? You were in Indiana."

"I asked my mother. She knows everything about everyone. She would call me after she got home from church and tell me all the gossip."

"Any of it good?"

"Well, the whole stolen-pie-recipe debacle of '71 was a huge thing. I learned entering a baking contest with a so-called stolen recipe will get you blacklisted in these parts."

"This is a world-renowned place of cowboys and outlaws, and now the biggest scandal is over a pie."

"People take their desserts very seriously around here. My mother also thinks you should hire some of the women who attend her church to bake for you on a rotating schedule. She says nothing beats home-cooked food made with love, and it would give the women a little pocket money of their own. At first I thought I was humoring her by telling you, but it's not a bad idea."

"You're right. It's actually a very good idea. It could be something that would draw people in. Can you have your mother make a list of her friends for me so I can reach out to them?"

"I can, but if you turn my mother loose, she'll have a dozen women signed up before dinnertime tonight. My mother taught kindergarten for thirty years, so if there's one thing she knows how to do, it's wrangle people."

"That sounds great."

"I also talked to my father and asked him for a list of reliable contractors. He gave me three. I called his top choice and set up a meeting for you tomorrow at ten. Is that a good time for you?"

"That's perfect. I wasn't expecting you to do all of that. You managed to get way more done than I have, and this is my restaurant. Thank you."

"I'm just doing my job. I worked as a bookkeeper for a busy salon to pay my way through grad school. You should probably look for an actual bookkeeper once you're fully opened. Managing the books for a place like this can be a lot. I can train someone before I leave."

He looked at her for a long moment. "Thinking about you leaving is the last thing I want to do right now."

She wasn't sure how to respond to that. He seemed almost sad, but he was probably overwhelmed with the number of things they needed to do. "Am I talking too much? I know it's a lot. I can leave you alone for a few hours. Just tell me when you're ready for more."

"You aren't talking too much. I'm glad you're here. I stopped by Randy's house this morning to share my news."

"I haven't seen him or Flora since they got back from their trip. He called my parents this morning and invited us all for dinner tonight. I'm pretty sure they're going to announce that they're having a baby."

Wyatt's eyes widened momentarily, and he turned around before she could read his expression.

"They told you this morning, didn't they?"

"I will not confirm or deny that. Come with me to the kitchen and help me check out the appliances. Depending on what needs to be repaired, we might have to move this budget around." He began walking away. She followed, but she wasn't done with the conversation yet.

"I can't believe he told you before he told us! When I see him, I'm going to yell at him."

"I never told you anything. So don't go yelling at anyone, champ. You aren't getting me in trouble. It seems to me you already knew."

"Oh, I knew a while ago. She was so sick at my graduation they almost had to leave. Plus, Randy kept touching her belly. They did a bad job hiding it."

"Do you want kids?" he asked her, taking her off guard.

"I think so. I'm not sure I would be a good mother though. I often find children loud and sticky."

"Fair points. I think people feel differently when they have their own."

"If I could have a quiet, non-sticky child, that would be great. What about you?"

"I'd have to find the right wife. It would all depend on her."

"I was half expecting you to tell me that you were getting married when you asked to see me."

He looked back. "Did you? Why? I haven't been dating anyone."

"I wasn't sure," she admitted. "I know you wrote me, but I figured there were things that you wanted to keep private."

"If I was dating someone I wanted to marry, I wouldn't have kept that from you. The woman I marry will be the most important person in my life. You're one of my oldest friends. I would absolutely never keep that from you."

"Are we really friends?"

"Why would you ask me that?" He seemed hurt by her question.

"Sometimes I wonder if you ever get past seeing me as Randy's little sister."

He looked at her for a long moment. "You are Randy's little sister, but you're also much more than that. You are a beautiful, intelligent woman, and I'm glad to have you in my life."

It was the sweetest thing anyone had ever said to her, and the foolish urge to hug him came over her in that moment. But she thought better of it. They were here to work. "Okay, friend. Let's inspect the appliances."

They checked the commercial refrigerator first. As soon as they walked in, a blast of cool air hit them. A quick check of the thermometer confirmed that it was at the right temperature.

They checked the microwave next. No issues.

They went over to the range. It was the most important appliance in the entire kitchen, with an oven, grill cooktop, and gas burners. No cooking got done without it.

Billie remembered it had been delivered the summer she went away to college. Wyatt's uncle had been nice enough to give her extra shifts so she could earn money for school. He would always slip her a few extra dollars here and there, telling her it was "a bonus." She smiled at the memory.

"What's the smile for?" Wyatt asked her.

"I was just thinking of when your uncle would give me extra tips the summer I was saving up for college. He took them right out of the register. It's no wonder he didn't want to give you the books. I'm pretty sure he never kept track of how much he gave me. Who knows who else he did that for?"

"Keeping track of things isn't Uncle John's bag. I can't find any documentation for it, but I remember when he ordered this range. He was so excited to get it. He said they could make twice as many pancakes for Sunday breakfast."

"Would you bring Sunday breakfast back?"

"I hadn't thought much about it. You think we should?"

"Only if it makes sense to you. But I loved coming here after church for brunch. It was the only time we all got to go out for a meal together. I can still remember you in your church clothes. You used to hate them so much, especially the shoes. It's ironic that you ended up in a career where you had to wear a suit every day."

"I still feel a little claustrophobic in dress clothes, but at least I get to pick my suits for work."

"You have good taste. I still can't get over how good you looked in that cream-colored suit you wore when you took us to that play in San Francisco. I felt like a bumpkin in comparison to you, but I'm grateful for that trip. I don't think I would have ever left Arizona to go to graduate school without it. You made me see that there was more to life than just this town."

"Did I make you feel bad when you came to visit me?"

"No, why?"

"You said you felt like a bumpkin. I never meant to make you feel that way. I just wanted you to have fun."

"I did have fun. You didn't do anything wrong. But let's face it, there was so much I didn't know about the world until I went on that trip. It opened my eyes to the possibility of having more."

"Is that why you applied for a job in New York? So you can have more?"

She shrugged. "I've applied a bunch of places. Each one could take me on a new adventure. Who knows what's out there for me?"

"Anything you want is out there for you," he said, and she heard heaviness in his voice, but she wasn't sure why. This conversation confused her. Wyatt fiddled with the knobs on the oven. It didn't work. No fire came from the stove. The grill didn't heat up. "Does this look like it's not all the way against the wall to you?"

"Yeah. Maybe it got moved when they cleaned behind there."

Wyatt pulled the stove away from the wall far enough so that they could walk behind it.

"The cord looks like it was chewed on."

"I don't think it was chewed on." He bent down and studied it. "It looks like someone tried to saw through this."

"Saw through it? Why wouldn't they just make a clean cut?"

He pulled a small jackknife out of his pocket and opened it up. "Because they were probably using something like this. The blade is too small to cut through without some serious elbow grease."

"Maybe it was just an accident. It could have gotten snagged when they moved it. It wasn't even plugged in. Maybe whoever moved it to clean back there damaged the cord and didn't say anything to your uncle because they didn't want to get in trouble. They probably figured it was the next owner's problem anyway."

"You're very optimistic, Billie. The power was shut off. The door was left wide open, and now the cord is cut. Those all can't be 'just accidents.'"

He walked away from her. Billie felt terrible. She wanted things to go smoothly for Wyatt. After seeing how detailed his plans were, she was sure this wasn't just a passing fancy.

ᐳ Chapter Four ᐸ

*By wisdom a house is built, and through understanding it is
established; through knowledge its rooms are filled
with rare and beautiful treasures.*
—Proverbs 24:3–4

"What do you think about moving the larger tables from this side to
the back?" Billie asked as she pointed to the layout he had sketched.
"We can fit three more two-seaters along this wall. Then the wait-
staff will have a little more clearance when they're leaving the
kitchen."

"With the addition of these three tables, that brings our seating
capacity to 280. By law, we can have three hundred people in here."

"Do you want to fill it? We can fit more tables here." She pointed
to the space in the restaurant they had delegated to be for private
parties. "But if you want the tables, the wagon won't fit there."

"You're right. I really want the wagon."

A week had gone by since they first started working on the
restaurant. Billie was proving to be more essential to him than he
could have ever imagined. Not only did she keep meticulous records,
but she made things happen quicker than he could fathom. They
had met with the contractor, applied for all the appropriate permits
and licensing, had the appliance repairmen out, and every lock

changed. There was no way he would have been able to get a tenth of that done without her.

The more he saw her in action, the more he knew that Randy was right. She was too talented to stay in Tombstone. There had to be a dozen job offers coming her way. She deserved every one of them. "You don't need any time off, do you? I didn't think to ask you if you had any plans this summer."

"No big plans. I wanted to spend some time with my family this summer before I left again to start my career."

"Do you have any more interviews coming up?"

"I had an offer, actually."

"A job offer?"

"Yes. There's a woman I met when I worked for the salon. It turns out her husband is an executive at a pharmaceutical company. I thought he was just going to look at my résumé and give me some feedback, but after I spoke to him on the phone, he offered me a job. I can be a budget analyst there or work as an accounting manager."

"Wow. That's amazing. Are you going to take it?"

"I don't know." She shrugged. "Indiana gets so cold in the winter. The salary isn't as high as the New York job, but it's much cheaper to live in the Midwest. He also offered me a substantial relocation stipend."

"You should seem happier about this."

"You'd think more choices would make a person happier. But it just makes for more thinking."

"When do you need to decide by?"

"He and his wife are going to Europe for a month, so I don't have to let him know until they return. I'm not sure I want to leave

Arizona just yet. Being back makes me realize how much I missed it here. I'm going to be an aunt. I don't want to miss out on that by being so far away. I don't think I can lure many people to Indianapolis to visit me either."

"I would come see you."

"Like all the other times you trekked out there when I was in grad school?"

"You never invited me," he said seriously. "I would have come."

She shook her head as if she didn't believe him. "Wherever you decide to work, I promise, I'll visit you," he said. "Especially if you go to New York. I'll help you find an apartment. I have some contacts there I can reach out to."

"I was leaning toward working in Phoenix. Why is it that the job I want the most is the one that won't let me know?"

"It's government. Everything moves slowly in government."

He heard the front door open, and both turned to look at the pair who walked in. There was a girl with one of the most impressive afros that Wyatt had ever seen and a young man who looked very much like her. "Hello," the girl said as she walked up to them, Wyatt could tell she was still in high school. "Mr. Keenan told me that you might be needing some help when your restaurant opens. I'm Renee, and this is my brother Donald. We would like to apply for jobs."

"I'm Billie, Mr. Keenan's sister," Billie said. "It's very nice to meet you. My brother must think very highly of you if he sent you here."

"He likes me because I can run fast," she said with a shy smile.

"You want to be a waitress?" Wyatt asked the girl.

"Sure. Or I can wash dishes or clean tables. Donald would like to work in the kitchen."

"Can you talk, Donald?" Wyatt asked him.

"Yes, sir. But sometimes it's easier when I let Renee do it for me." He grinned. "I've worked in a kitchen before. I helped cook in my uncle's restaurant in New Orleans, but there was a fire, and the restaurant closed."

"You're both hired. The restaurant won't be open for a little while, but we need help getting it ready. Can you come back on Monday? I have a delivery coming. We're going to need help."

"Yes, Mr. Clark," Renee said. "Thank you."

As soon as the words left Renee's mouth, they heard the sound of glass shattering. Instinctively, Wyatt grabbed Billie and pulled her behind him.

"The window," she gasped. The big front window of the restaurant was now in a thousand tiny pieces on the floor. Wyatt walked forward, Donald behind him. They looked out to see if anyone or anything was outside. The parking lot was empty. Inside, a rock lay amongst the shards of glass. Not a big rock, but one big enough to shatter the window.

"This definitely isn't a coincidence." Wyatt turned and looked back at Billie. The open door, the cut cord, the power that was switched off. Someone was out to get him.

"I heard there are some kids going around causing trouble," Donald said.

"What kind of trouble?" Billie asked him.

"Mostly small stuff. Throwing eggs. Knocking over people's mailboxes. I overheard our neighbor talking about it with my mom. This seems like something they might do."

"Do you have any idea who these kids might be?" Wyatt asked.

"No, but I heard they looked young. Maybe thirteen or fourteen."

"Maybe we should ask around," Billie suggested. "See if any of the other business owners had anything happen. It's not a bad idea for us to talk to them in general. We're going to need their support."

"You're right, but we need to take care of this window first. Donald, Renee, can you start working right now?"

"We can," Renee answered.

"Good. Donald, I need you to come with me to the hardware store. We're going to board up the window. Renee, would you help sweep up the glass?"

"Sure."

"Should I call the police?" Billie asked. "I feel like we need to make a report."

"You should. Can you check our insurance policy? I'm not sure if this will be covered."

"Yes. And I'll call around to see if we can get the glass replaced before the end of the week."

"I know exactly what you need to board up a window, Mr. Clark," Donald said as they walked into the hardware store. "I had to cover the windows of my uncle's restaurant during Hurricane Carmen two years ago. Do you have tools at the restaurant?"

"Probably not," he said, hearing the frustration in his voice. "My uncle probably cleared those out when he closed down."

"You worked in your uncle's restaurant too?"

"I did. It's lucky for me that you walked into the Rusty Spur when you did. Now I have a cook who can board up windows. Go ahead and grab whatever tools you think we'll need for the restaurant in general. I need to talk to the owner about the wood."

Donald nodded and went off to complete his task.

Mr. Johnson, who'd owned the store since Wyatt was a kid, came down one of the aisles and smiled as soon as he saw him. "Hello, Wyatt. My son told me you were back in town. Rumor is that you're reopening the Rusty Spur."

"I'm trying. I'm here for some plywood. A rock was thrown through the restaurant's front window just a few minutes ago."

"That's terrible. I have exactly what you need to board it up." He motioned Wyatt to follow him. "Did you see who it was?"

"No. We were in the middle of hiring staff. Next thing we knew the window was shattered."

"Do you think it could be kids? I've had a few customers come in needing replacement mailboxes."

"The teens I just hired told me the same thing."

"This type of thing happens every few years. Kids playing mailbox baseball, doing doughnuts on someone's lawn. A little mischief is one thing. Destroying property is going too far. If you find the kids who did it, you need to have them scrub toilets in your restaurant until they repay the repair costs."

"That's not a bad idea. Maybe it'll teach them a lesson."

"I'm glad you're opening up the Rusty Spur. The town isn't the same without it. I used to take the wife every Friday night. We miss it."

"We're planning to be open by Labor Day. Hopefully, we won't run into any more unexpected issues."

"That's life when you run your own business. Just when you think things are going smoothly, a bump in the road appears and slows you down." Mr. Johnson showed him the plywood he had in stock. What they needed to cover the window was too big to fit in Wyatt's car, so Mr. Johnson had his son load it in their pickup truck and drop it off at the restaurant while Wyatt finished paying for their purchases.

"Thank you for your help today, Mr. Johnson. We'll be back soon. I'm going to need to order some paint."

"I'll be here for you. Thank you for shopping locally. They're building that resort up the hill, but they haven't come to see me once. They're trucking everything in from out of town. The owners haven't even bothered to meet anyone else here. No one knows who they are for sure, but it would be in their best interest to start building relationships. We business owners need to stick together."

Mr. Johnson's words were very similar to Billie's. Wyatt was back home now. He was staying for good. He needed to get to know the other business owners. The resort was probably a good thing for the town, and anything that brought in more tourists was welcome, but something about it troubled him. They had been building for well over a year and nobody had met the owners? It was odd.

"Maybe I should go and look it over," he said.

Mr. Johnson grinned. "I'm very curious to see what it looks like. I might have to take a trip over there myself someday."

Billie and Renee had just finished sweeping up the last of the glass when Wyatt and Donald walked back in. Billie could feel how tense Wyatt was. Things had been going so well this past week, which had made her put what happened that first night out of her head. But this worried her.

"Were you able to make those calls?" he asked her.

"Come on, Renee," Donald said to his sister. "Help me board the window."

"I can do that, Donald," Wyatt said to him. "Renee doesn't have to."

"I know how, Mr. Clark," she said. "You talk to Ms. Keenan." She walked out with her brother.

"I wasn't able to make the calls, and you're not going to be happy when I tell you why."

He looked pained for a moment. "I'm almost afraid to ask, but tell me anyway."

"The phones aren't working. I tried the one in the kitchen, the one in the office, and the one in your apartment. I couldn't get a dial tone."

Wyatt rubbed his temples. "This is not good. How can we get this done without a working phone?"

She felt terrible. She wanted so much for this restaurant to be what he had dreamed. She wanted it so much, it had started to feel like her dream. She grabbed his hand and squeezed his fingers. "We'll get this done. I promise you."

He pulled her into a hug and rested his chin on her hair. "You promise, huh?"

"I have faith. These are only small bumps in the road."

They were quiet for a moment. She shut her eyes and leaned against him. It was such a different sensation being hugged by him. He was large and warm and solid. He was her brother's friend, but this hug didn't feel brotherly. He was her friend. They had probably been true friends outside of their connection to Randy for a long time.

"Wyatt, are you okay?"

"Uncle John?" He pulled away from Billie, and she immediately felt the absence of his security. "I'm fine. Why are you here?"

"Bernie Anderson overheard you when you were in the hardware store. He called and told me that someone threw a rock through the window. I tried to call here, but I couldn't get an answer, so I came down to see if you were okay."

"We're fine. Just out a window."

"Hello, Billie," Mr. Clark greeted her. "I didn't recognize you at first. I was visiting my wife's family when you came home for Christmas."

"Hello, Mr. Clark." She walked over to hug him.

"Uncle John," he corrected her. "You and Randy are family. Your mother told me you got offered a big job in New York. What are you doing here in the restaurant?"

"I'm helping Wyatt for the summer. I wanted to spend some time with my family and think about my job offers before I made a decision."

"She's got two good offers already, Uncle John. Billie is a genius. They're going to be fighting over her."

"Of course they are." He smiled at her, and then turned his attention back to Wyatt. "I have a connection with a glass guy. I'll have him come out tomorrow."

"We were going to call the insurance company," Wyatt told him. "And then probably call around for quotes."

"You could do that, but sometimes knowing a guy is quicker and easier than going through the process. Let me take care of this for you."

"The window we can handle, Uncle John. What I'd like is your feedback about the plans for this place."

"Nope. The glass is where I draw the line. I'm out of the restaurant business. I'm in the sleep-late, go-out-on-weekends, and not-come-home-smelling-like-french-fries business now. You should be too. We did all that work to send you away to college and law school, and now you come back here and follow in our footsteps."

Billie didn't miss the disappointment in Uncle John's tone. He wasn't helping Wyatt, because he was retired. He wasn't helping Wyatt, because he didn't want him living the same life he had.

"You act like you and Dad were criminals. You ran the largest restaurant in Tombstone."

"I'm not ashamed. But your father is gone, and I'm tired. So, you have fun with this, but I need to be done."

"I understand," Wyatt said, but Billie wasn't sure he did. He might have a neutral expression on his face, but she knew how hard it was for him to hear his uncle's words.

"Good. Come over for dinner this week. Billie, you come too."

Wyatt nodded but didn't say anything else. His uncle left soon after.

"Do you want me to go up the road to see if the other businesses have phone service? Or I can go to the police station and make a report?"

"You can take the rest of the day off, Billie. I'm going to go check on how Donald and Renee are coming with the window, and then I'm going for a drive. I need to clear my head for a bit."

He walked outside, leaving her alone in the restaurant. This had started as a way for her to pass some time and earn extra funds before her move, but it had become more important to her than she could have expected. She believed in this place. None of the things that had happened so far were connected, in her opinion. She really did believe they were a string of coincidences, and in the grand scheme of things, relatively minor. She didn't want to think that this place was doomed, but if Wyatt believed that, then there wasn't a chance that they would make it to opening. She was going to have to figure out what to do to ensure they did.

Wyatt thought Billie had listened to him and gone home for the day, but he should have known better. She had left only for about an hour or so. He helped Renee and Donald patch up the window, and then the two teens went around the grounds of the restaurant, picking up trash. He didn't ask them to. They just saw it needed to be done and did it. They found a bunch of gum wrappers and a few baseball cards, which confirmed to Wyatt that kids definitely hung out in the parking lot. It made sense for it to be kids. Causing chaos for chaos's sake. Throwing a rock through a window didn't seem like something an adult would do in broad daylight. The probability of getting caught was just too high.

He needed to make sure he was more vigilant. Or at least find a way to let people know that the restaurant was being watched at all times. This place was too important to him. This was his home. He felt comfortable here, but he couldn't feel too comfortable.

When Billie walked back into the restaurant, she carried a bag full of food. Donald and Renee appeared behind her a moment later as if they had smelled the food from across the parking lot.

"I got lunch," she said, smiling at him. "I spoke to Mrs. Swanson, who has a son who works for the phone company. He's coming by to check the phones this afternoon. I also called Pete Jackson. You remember him? He was in my grade in high school. He works for the marshal's office." She put the bag on the counter and started to pull out the contents. "He's been a deputy for five years now. I mentioned what happened to the window, and he confirmed that there are a group of minors running around causing trouble, but it's mostly been in the evening. He said you can go down to the marshal's office and file an official report. I couldn't file one. It's not my property."

"You were supposed to be taking the afternoon off."

"You trying to get out of paying me?" she countered. "Also, what am I supposed to do all day when I know there are things to be done here? We all need to eat anyway. Renee and Donald, I wasn't sure what you like, so I got a little bit of everything."

"Look at all those snack cakes, Renee," Donald said. He grabbed one off the table, unwrapped it, and shoved the whole thing into his mouth.

"Our mom won't buy these," Renee said. "She says she can make a cake that tastes better and is cheaper."

"Yeah," Donald said with his mouth full, "but getting her to bake is like pulling teeth. She'll only do it on the holidays. Plus, these are good. You got Moon Pies? There's a banana cake!"

"You'll have to excuse my brother. He gets very excited when it comes to snacks or food in general," Renee said.

"Then today's your lucky day. I stopped by the Ghost Town Grill and got steak sandwiches and fries. I also got a tuna salad, a turkey, a ham and cheese, and a roast beef."

"There's enough food to feed ten people here," Wyatt exclaimed. "How much did you spend on all of this? Let me pay you back."

"Mrs. Swanson gave everything to me for five dollars. So when she comes here to eat with her large family, and she will because I made sure to tell her to bring them opening weekend, we will give her a discount. The business owners in town have to look out for each other. You have to build a community here."

That was the third time today he'd heard that. Billie had proved that being friendly to the people in town got you places.

"You also don't have any food in your apartment. I figured you could eat leftovers tonight."

"Now you're worried about my meals as well?" he asked. "That's not in your job description."

"I don't have a job description." She turned away from him and started walking back to the office area. "Everyone eat. The fries are getting cold. Cold fries are the worst."

Wyatt grabbed two sandwiches and followed her as the kids dug into their food. She was sitting at the desk when he walked in.

"You didn't take anything to eat," he said, tossing a sandwich on the desk.

"I wanted to let the kids get what they wanted first."

"Donald inhaled half a steak sandwich in one bite. I don't think he's one of those kids you leave food around."

"You were like that. Especially after football practice. It was lucky your family owned a restaurant. You could eat a whole roasted chicken in five minutes."

"Eat. You were here before nine this morning, and you haven't stopped all day."

He sat down opposite her and opened his sandwich. When she saw it was tuna, she stood up, took the sandwich out of his hand, and gave him the one she had.

He started adding things up. She remembered he didn't like tuna. She brought him extra food because she knew he didn't have any. She was working even though he'd sent her home. She was taking care of him. He had been alone in another state a thousand miles away and had taken care of himself completely since he had gone away to college. But he had to admit, it was nice to have someone else care, although he feared she was doing too much. He didn't know how to return the favor. And what was worse, he was starting to depend on her. He was going to have to let her go in two short months. He needed to pull back from her, but he had no idea how that was going to be possible.

"You don't have to sit in here with me," she said to him just before she bit into her sandwich. "I thought you needed space to clear your head."

"Why didn't you go home then?"

"I already told you why. If I go home and think about all the things I have to do, I'll go into an anxious tailspin. I can't sit and watch *General Hospital* with my mother and pretend like I don't have a to-do list that's forty-five items long. You don't need to feel obligated to be here just because I am. You can take a break."

"Why are you working so hard? This is my restaurant. These are my problems. I originally intended for you to just do the accounting, but you're doing more than I am."

"No I'm not. You have the plan. I put it into action."

"You fix the plan, add to it, put it into action, and make a new one."

"Am I annoying you?"

She was doing the exact opposite. The more she was around, the more he wanted to be around her. He thought about her when she left in the evening. He couldn't wait to see her in the morning. It was getting bad. "Will you go with me somewhere?"

"Depends on where this somewhere is."

"It's a resort."

She gave him a smile that he could only describe as flirty. "You taking me on a vacation?"

"You say the word, and I'll take you anywhere you want to go. But, unfortunately, this resort is right up the road."

Her eyes went wide with excitement, and she let out a small gasp. "Of course I'll go with you. I've been dying to see what it looks like. No one in town has any idea what's going on up there."

"Well, we're going to be the first to know. Let me pay the kids for the day, and then we'll drive up there."

Twenty minutes later they were on their way to the resort. It was massive compared to what they had in town. There were a few hotels and motels for tourists, but they'd never had a full-service resort before. Whoever had designed it had paid attention to the details. It looked as if they time-traveled back a hundred years to the 1870s. The road wasn't paved like it was in the rest of the town. Instead, it was dirt, reddish-brown in color. There was a stable for horses on one side, a small pasture for cattle on the other. There was a replica wagon parked in front of the main building. It looked to be fully functional and much bigger than the one they had secured for decoration at the Rusty Spur.

"This place looks amazing," Billie said in awe. "Whoever owns it has substantial funds."

"I don't think anyone knows who owns it. When I talked to Mr. Johnson at the hardware store, he implied that the owners were a mystery to everyone."

"Their workers don't come into town. They must be feeding and housing them here."

"They certainly have the space to do it. I remember when the town sold this piece of land. It's over a hundred acres."

Wyatt pulled his car to a stop in front of the wagon and got out. It was a hot day, well over a hundred degrees. The only thing he would miss about San Francisco was not feeling as if his skin was on fire every time he stepped outdoors. Billie got out on her side. She wore brown leather sandals and a burgundy sundress with little white flowers on it. In the direct sun he could see the very light dusting of freckles sprinkled across her nose. It was hard to pull his eyes away from her.

"Excuse me," a man said as they walked through the door. "We aren't open for business yet."

"We know," Wyatt said, extending his hand. "I'm Wyatt Clark, and this is Billie Keenan. We're from the Rusty Spur. We just wanted to welcome you to town."

"The owner of the Rusty Spur? I thought it was closed."

"It was. My uncle has retired. I took over, and we're doing some renovations. We're planning to open Labor Day Weekend."

"That's news to me. My name is Dave Michael. I'm the manager of this place."

"Are the owners here? The business owners in town like to get together from time to time and discuss how everyone can help each other," Billie said. "We would love to invite them to join us."

Wyatt looked at her for a moment. He had no idea what she was talking about.

Dave paused a moment before answering. "The owners are off-site. They only come in once a month or so to check on our progress."

"Who are the owners?" Wyatt asked, feeling like Dave was hiding something.

"The owners are just some people who dreamed of opening a resort and are finally able to put that plan into action. But I'll be sure to pass along the information to them about the business owners in Tombstone helping each other out. They would appreciate the welcome."

"Please do," Billie said, glancing at Wyatt before looking around. "This place is quite impressive. I'm sure you've been working non-stop to get it completed. When do you plan to open?"

"September," Dave said. "Labor Day weekend. It looks like we'll have competing openings."

"That's very soon. How are you managing to get it all done? We haven't seen anyone who works here in town. If I didn't know better, I'd say you were using magic."

"No magic. Just a team of workers we brought in. They're living in the staff quarters while they complete the job."

"They don't come to town for food or entertainment?" Wyatt asked.

"We have a cook on staff. We get weekly deliveries of everything she needs. Once a month we take the workers to Tucson so they can have some downtime."

"You aren't interested in hiring local guys?" Wyatt asked. "It would save you the trouble of feeding and transporting your own."

"This works for us," Dave said. "Our men tend to work faster when there are no distractions from their personal lives."

"The amount you've accomplished in such a short time is very impressive, Dave." Billie smiled and flipped her hair. Wyatt didn't like it. Not that he had a right not to like it, but he had a feeling he knew what Billie was up to. "I would love it if you gave us a tour. Before Wyatt came back home, he was an attorney in San Francisco. He still has close ties with his former clients there. I know some of them would love to visit a place like this in Tombstone and live out their Old West fantasies."

"It's funny you should say that. There's a market for people from the city, you know, business types, who want to work on a ranch. We're offering a 'Cowboy Experience' package. It will include moving cattle, fixing fences, currying horses, and whatever else needs to be done around here."

"You mean to tell me you'll charge people to work as ranch hands?" Wyatt asked.

"Yes, and people are willing to pay a pretty penny for it. Can you believe it? There's a sucker born every minute."

"I bet that was your idea, Dave," Billie said. "It's brilliant. Please show us around. We definitely know people who would be interested."

"It's hard to say no to a beautiful woman. I can show you the main building."

They followed him farther inside the air-conditioned lobby. It smelled like wood and something musky that Wyatt couldn't place, but overall, the smell was pleasant. The outside might look like a replica of Tombstone in the 1800s, but the inside had all the modern amenities of the 1970s. The walls were lined in rich, printed wallpaper. The furniture was clearly new, but it was made to look like antiques. There were photographs of Wyatt Earp and Doc Holliday on the side tables, and beautiful brass light fixtures that Wyatt would love to have in the restaurant. The front desk was old-fashioned in style, made of dark wood and polished to a high gloss. It was clear that this wasn't some cheaply thrown-together place. Thought had gone into every inch of it.

"This is our lobby. We're going to have our staff dress in Old West clothing to give our guests a more complete experience."

"That sounds like fun," Billie said, encouraging Dave to keep talking.

"I'll show you some of our rooms next. First up is our Cowboy Bunkhouse. This is for the customer who really wants a rugged experience. And by rugged, I mean the beds are twin size. This is a two-room suite with a shared bathroom."

It was minimally decorated with sand-colored painted walls and wood furniture. The only spots of color were from the brightly patterned quilts on the bed.

He then showed them more typical hotel rooms that were tastefully decorated and designed for guests who liked to relax. They passed the pool, which was still in the process of being built, and ended up in the restaurant. Compared to everything else, it was almost a letdown. It was large, an open plan, plenty of room for over a hundred guests, but it was just a bunch of tables and chairs. There was a wagon wheel on one wall and some photographs of Saguaro National Park on another.

"Are you offering breakfast here?" Billie asked.

"Yes, daily from eight to ten. We'll have the basics—eggs, toast, bacon, and oatmeal. Lunch will be from twelve to two. We'll do a full-service dinner from five to nine. What about you guys?"

"We only do breakfast on Sundays," Billie answered. "But we'll be open from eleven to ten every day."

"What kind of food will you be serving?"

Wyatt started to speak, but Billie cut him off. "Good old-fashioned American comfort food."

"Makes sense. You're staying open that late? Are you going to be having any nighttime activities?"

"We haven't figured that out yet," she said, even though they said they were going to bring back line dancing on Thursday nights. "We still need to figure out staffing. Are you going to be hiring locally?"

"For some of the positions. Others we'll bring in from outside of town."

"Judging by the size of this place, you're going to need an army to staff it," Wyatt said. "But I'm sure if you can't find enough people, you can always get your customers to do the housekeeping and tell them it's a part of the package."

Dave laughed. "That's not a bad idea."

"Thank you so much for your time, Dave," Billie said as they headed toward the entrance. "We know you must have a lot of work to do. Please come visit us. The local business owners would love to meet you."

"I will come visit. Thank you for the invite."

"Oh," Wyatt said, turning back around. "There've been some minor vandalism issues cropping up in town. Have you had any problems with anything like that?"

"No, we haven't. What kind of things are you talking about?"

"Nothing major. Some broken mailboxes. Rock throwing. Kid stuff. No one has gotten a clear look at any of the culprits, but I thought I'd warn you so you can keep a lookout."

"Rock throwing? I'm guessing something was damaged due to that. That kind of thing could cost a pretty penny. Thanks for letting me know. I'll be sure to tell my security guys."

They said their goodbyes and walked back to Wyatt's car.

"There's something about that guy that's a little off. I don't think I trust him," Billie said.

"I don't think he feels the same way as you. You got a lot more information out of him than I ever would have alone. He let it all out."

"A little flattery and a smile go a long way. Men like women to think they're strong and smart. I let him think I thought he was strong and smart, and it worked."

"Do you do that to me? Make me think I'm strong and smart to get what you want?"

"You *are* strong and smart," she said matter-of-factly. "Besides, I don't want anything from you, and if I did, I would ask you for it."

"I wish you would ask me for something. I'm starting to feel like I'll never be able to repay you for all you're doing."

"You are literally paying me to work for you. I also like having you indebted to me. That way you can't say no when I ask you for a really big favor."

"How big of a favor?"

"A kidney." She grinned. "Something on that scale."

"Is that all?" He grinned back.

"I also didn't get all the information from him. He never said who the owners are. He purposely didn't. Why is it so secretive?"

"That struck me as odd too. And do the business owners meet once a month? I've never heard about it."

"They don't formally meet all at once, but it's not a bad idea to start a business association. When I worked in Indianapolis, all the business owners met regularly to discuss how they could work together. We should do that here. We could even have the meetings at the Rusty Spur. I've been thinking about this all week, but I didn't bring it up because we have enough to do right now."

"We do. But it's a good idea. I'll suggest it to some of the other owners in town." He started his car and pulled off.

"The restaurant here isn't anywhere as good as the Rusty Spur will be. They have a bland decor, limited hours, and I'm pretty sure they'll have basic food."

"In theory, the Rusty Spur will be better, but we're a long way from opening, and today set us back a little."

"Just a tiny bit. We hired two staff members and met the competition."

"There's more than one restaurant in town. We have way more competition than this resort."

She waved her hand dismissively. "The other places aren't anything compared to what we're going to do. If we were opening a resort, I might be worried, but we can make a better restaurant."

"You made sure you didn't give him any specifics about our plans."

"He looks like the type that might borrow our ideas and use them for his own place. We can't risk that. We can pull a lot of his customers away from here for dinner and Sunday breakfast."

"You're right. He didn't seem to know that we were opening back up. My uncle said that he spoke to someone from the resort about their buying the Rusty Spur to use as an event space. We're the closest restaurant to them."

"Why wouldn't they just build their own place? They have the land for it."

"It might be cheaper for them to renovate the existing space."

"It's actually a smart plan. Stinks for them you aren't selling."

CHAPTER FIVE

Do not conform to the pattern of this world, but be transformed
by the renewing of your mind.
—Romans 12:2

In the week that followed their visit to the new resort, Billie and Wyatt put their plans into overdrive. They hired most of the staff, including Maureen, a waitress who had worked for Wyatt's uncle up until she had her first child, and Chip, who had been a cook at the restaurant since they were kids.

"I can't believe you managed to lure Chip out of retirement," Billie said to Wyatt as they carried trays of food to the tables in the private-party section of the restaurant.

"It didn't take much convincing. I asked him if he'd consider working the dinnertime shift on the weekends. He countered with working all the lunch shifts and Sunday morning. He says he has to be home to see *The Carol Burnett Show*."

"I don't blame him. She's hysterical."

"I forgot how heavy these trays are," Wyatt said as they neared the table. "I haven't done this in almost a decade."

"You're getting old," she teased. "This is nothing."

"You sure you two don't need any help?" Randy asked. They were doing a tasting tonight. Wyatt had dozens of ideas for what he wanted to go on the menu. But they couldn't have it all, so tonight they were going to sample everything and decide what should stay and what needed to go.

"You're our guests tonight," Wyatt responded. "All I need from you is your honest opinion."

"I think I can handle that." Randy rubbed Flora's back. "How are you doing, sweetheart? I know smells can bother you sometimes."

"I think I'm fine. It's only eggs that are bothering me this week. Last week it was beef. I'll be glad when this part of my pregnancy is over." Flora was just starting to show, her belly slightly curving. Billie was so happy that God blessed them with this baby.

"We don't have any eggs tonight," Wyatt told her. "We're going to do this again with the breakfast menu in a few days. You might want to sit that one out."

"I go from starving to sick. Who knows how I'll feel in a few days, but please keep inviting me. It's very exciting for us to be included in this. I know you aren't finished yet, but I can't get over how beautiful it looks in here already."

They'd had the floors refinished and stained a rich cinnamon. Wyatt had found another restaurant that was going out of business and was able to get tables and chairs for the back section of the restaurant for half of what they'd expected to pay. The chairs were made out of wooden barrels, handcrafted by an artist in Arizona. Billie had never seen anything like them. Wyatt always gave her too much credit for this place coming together, but he had a vision that she could never possess. He saw beauty in places that others would overlook. He had imagination. She hadn't known this about him before. It was odd knowing someone for your entire life and finding out there was still so much to learn about them.

"I'm starving. Where is everyone?" Randy asked.

"Mom and Dad should be here by now." Billie grabbed Wyatt's wrist and glanced at his watch.

"This is just the appetizer round," Wyatt said as he arranged the plates on the table. We should probably start before they get cold. Some of these are basic starters that a lot of people have had before, like stuffed mushrooms, but we put a spin on a few things. Try the chicken wings first. Donald made the sauce."

Randy grabbed one and took a bite. "You have got to keep this," he said. "You said Donald made this? He's just a kid."

"He's a kid who can cook. I was worried about finding someone who could execute what I wanted, but I think he's got it. He loves food. He might eat into my profit, but that's okay as long as he keeps cooking."

They also tried barbecue meatballs and chicken kabobs. All three were voted to go on the menu. The next thing Wyatt presented them with was a skillet corn bread. He cut a piece for Randy and Flora and then handed them a ramekin of butter.

"You have to try this, Billie," he said. "I sampled it in the kitchen. I think it might be my favorite." He slathered butter on top of the rest of the corn bread in the skillet, stuck a fork in it, and fed her a bite. "It's jalapeño cheddar. We're so close to Mexico, I have to incorporate some of that influence in the food."

She closed her eyes for a moment as the flavors flooded her. Sweet, spicy, salty, perfect. "You have to keep that stuff away from me. I won't be able to fit through the door by the end of the year."

"It's a keeper, right?" He smiled at her softly and lifted his thumb to wipe a crumb off her chin.

"What's going on with you two?" Randy huffed. There was a definite frown on his face.

"What do you mean?" Billie asked.

"He's feeding you. In fact, you both have been very…" He paused as if he couldn't find the word. "Close."

"You jealous, Randy?" Wyatt grinned at him. "I can feed you some corn bread too."

"I'll pass." He looked back and forth between them suspiciously. Billie didn't know what to say, so she said nothing. She hadn't thought anything of it when Wyatt fed her, but it wasn't something many friends would do. It was an intimate action. "You sure nothing is going on with you two?" Randy asked again.

"I'm fond of your sister," Wyatt said. "She's my friend, and there's no way I could have done any of this without her. I've seen more of her than anyone else this past month. So yes, we're close. I'm not sure how she feels about me, but I'm starting to think I can't live without her." He leaned over and kissed Billie's cheek. "I'm going to check on the next round." He got up and left, and Billie sat there, stunned, for a moment.

"He's messing with you," she said, but she wasn't sure if she was talking to herself or to her brother.

"Oh really?" Flora said with a grin. "He sounded serious to me. He *looks* serious to me."

"I'm not sure I like the way he was looking at her," Randy grumbled.

"He looks at her like she's a beautiful creature descended from heaven."

"Stop it, you two." Billie's cheeks felt hot, and she hoped it didn't show on her face. "I work for him. I'm good at my job. All my bosses feel that way about me. I think you're jealous that I stole your best friend."

"You actually did steal my best friend. Now give me something of yours."

"Ha! I don't have anything good to give you."

"You're going to babysit for us and do our taxes next year."

"Only if you pay me."

"Pay you!"

"Yes. Wyatt does. Why do you think I'm here?"

"Billie?" She heard her mother's voice coming from the front of the restaurant.

"We're back here." She was relieved her mother showed up when she did. It would put a stop to the conversation about her and Wyatt. The restaurant was coming together and would open soon. Then there would be no place for her here. She didn't want to think about that. She'd gotten used to seeing him every day.

Her mother was a little more dressed up than usual. She wore a long, flowing paisley skirt with a white short-sleeved top. "You look pretty, Mom."

"Thank you." She smiled. "We don't get out much. I felt like getting a little fancier tonight."

"Hey!" Billie's father said as he walked up to them. "Are you going to compliment my outfit?"

"You look lovely too, Dad. Come sit. We have appetizers out now. So far everything is staying on the menu."

"You don't have to tell me twice." He greeted Randy and Flora and sat down at the table. He looked around for a long moment.

Billie wasn't sure why she held her breath as he did. The restaurant was far from done, but after all the work they'd put in, she really wanted him to like it. "It feels like we're in a different place," he finally said. "When I heard that Wyatt was reopening the restaurant, I thought he literally was just going to flip on the lights and go back to business as usual."

"It would have been too easy to do that, Mr. Keenan," Wyatt said, returning from the kitchen.

"Call me William. You're an adult now. I promise you, it's okay." He grinned at him. "It feels classy in here. Are you going to allow kids?" he asked.

"Of course," Billie answered. "This a family town."

"Are you going to have a menu for children?"

Wyatt and Billie looked at each other. "We didn't think of that," Wyatt said.

"Good thing I'm here," her father said. "I guess that means I eat free for life!"

"Hello?" They heard a man's voice. Wyatt frowned and walked toward the front. Billie excused herself and followed him. They spotted Dave, the manager of the resort, walking through the door.

Billie could feel Wyatt tense up. She stepped in front of him. "Hi, Dave. What brings you here?"

"I was just taking you up on your invitation to visit while I was in town." He looked around for a long moment, taking everything in. "I saw cars in the parking lot and lights on. I figured you must have something going on tonight."

It was a Friday night. They weren't open for business yet. There was no reason to expect them to be there at this time.

"Billie's family is here," Wyatt said to him. "We're having a little get-together."

"That's nice," Dave said, his eyes still on the surroundings. "This place is much bigger than I expected. Is it a three-hundred-seater?"

"Yeah. Give or take a few."

"Floors look good. I see you don't have all your tables yet. Where are you getting them from? I have a wholesaler I could put you in contact with."

"We're sourcing the furniture locally," Billie told him. "Everything in the Rusty Spur will come from the area."

"Except the food." Dave laughed. "Unless you've got some fish tanks in the back. Who's your supplier? Our chef wants to put fish on the menu. This is a landlocked state. Everything is coming here frozen."

"We haven't gotten there yet," Wyatt told him. "We're still weighing our options."

"If you wait too long, you might not have food in time for your opening."

"Good advice," Billie said. "We'll get on that."

"You ever think of putting a stage over there?" He pointed to the space where the counter was. "You'd lose some seating, but you could have live music on the weekends."

"Traditionally, we've been slammed on the weekends. We can't give up the space for a permanent stage."

"You were slammed on the weekends? I heard the business slowed down here the last couple of years."

"I was away, and my uncle was getting ready to retire. I'm expecting that things will pick up when we reopen under my ownership."

Dave looked directly at Wyatt for the first time since he walked in. "Yeah. I'm sure it will. I'll let you get back to your family function."

He walked out without another word. "He was here to spy," Wyatt huffed. "There's something slimy about that guy. I don't trust him."

"To be fair, we kind of went there to spy too."

"We weren't spying. We went during the day and asked for a tour. This guy shows up at night. For what reason? He had no reason to think we were here. He's up to something. I don't believe for one second that he's trying to offer friendly advice."

"There are other restaurants in town. Why would he care about us?" Billie didn't want to think that Dave had nefarious plans, but even she had to admit there was something off with his visit.

"I don't know, but I don't trust that guy," Wyatt repeated. "We need to stay extra vigilant."

The next morning Wyatt woke up in the apartment over the restaurant feeling like he'd gotten no sleep at all. Everyone had stayed late. Billie didn't leave till almost midnight. Wyatt's mother had ended up coming to the tasting soon after they brought the entrées out. They'd gotten a lot accomplished, and the menu was set.

His mother had been surprisingly supportive. He knew she hadn't been on board at first because she didn't want him giving up his career. He also knew it had been hard for her to come to the restaurant since his father died. But if she was sad last night, she didn't let on. She seemed to be enjoying herself with Billie's family. He couldn't remember the last time they had all been together. There was a warmth in the room that he had been missing all the years he was away. He hadn't realized that was what the emptiness was in his life. He had missed being a part of a family.

It would have been nearly a perfect night even with Dave's unexpected visit, but his uncle's absence was weighing on him. Uncle John hadn't spoken to him since the day he'd stopped by the restaurant. He stayed true to his word and had his guy come fix the window. He had even paid for it, but that was where his support stopped. He made it clear that he wanted no part of the new Rusty Spur. This place had become such a huge part of Wyatt's life. Nearly all his thoughts surrounded it. He wanted to share that with the man who was a second father to him, but he couldn't, and he would have to get over that.

He hated to sit alone and stew in his own troubled thoughts, so he got dressed and left the restaurant, which was now his home. He didn't know what to do with himself. He went to the diner and picked up some breakfast. Instead of taking it back to the restaurant, he drove to Billie's house—technically her parents' house. She lived in the in-law apartment that her grandmother had lived in when they were kids. It had its own separate entrance. He hadn't been inside this part of the house in probably twenty years. As soon as he lifted his hand to knock on the door, it opened. Billie stood there, looking at him curiously with her head tilted to one side. She was adorable this morning in an Arizona State T-shirt and a pair of shorts. Her feet were bare. Her curls were wild. This was how he had known her when they were teenagers. Not so polished and put together. He had to admit she was more beautiful now than he had ever seen her.

"We aren't working today," she said.

"No. We aren't. But I have too much breakfast. Leftover breakfast isn't great, so I figured I would share it with someone."

"I'm that someone?"

"You're always that someone," he said, not meaning to but also meaning every word of it.

"Come in." She stepped aside. Much of the apartment looked the same as the last time he saw it. Right out of the '50s. The couch was a pastel blue. The curtains were white and breezy. It didn't look like a typical desert-style home. Billie's grandmother had been from Pennsylvania and had brought her style with her. But he also saw some new additions. There were a couple of macrame hangings on the wall. A shag throw rug was under the coffee table, and a rattan shelf held plants and books.

It made sense for her not to fully redecorate, because she was supposed to be moving away in less than a month. They hadn't talked about her career choices in a few weeks. He burned with curiosity to know where she would pick, but he couldn't bring himself to ask her again. Part of him didn't want to know because then he would have to face that whatever it was that was going on with them this summer was ending. He didn't want to think about that.

"You've saved me from eating Malt-O-Meal this morning."

"Malt-O-Meal?" He set the food on her small kitchen table. "Could you have picked a more boring cereal? Now they've got Kaboom with clowns and Fruit Brute with marshmallows."

"I would love those, but I'm no longer seven, and I feel like I should be a little more mature in my cereal choices. Isn't that stuff all sugar anyway?"

"Yes, but take a walk on the wild side once in a while."

She smiled and shook her head before turning away to get plates and forks from the kitchen. "Did you take a walk on the wild side with your breakfast choice?"

"No. After we ate all that food last night, I decided to go for a light breakfast of cottage cheese and fruit salad."

Billie paused and turned back to look at him. Her face said it all.

He couldn't contain his laughter. "I got a western omelet with a side of potatoes and toast."

"Good." She sat down at the table and put a plate in front of him. "I hate to waste food, but I was going to tell you to share that cottage cheese with the trash can. I cannot stand that stuff."

"My mom used to eat it with pineapple every morning. She probably still does. I can't stand even the look of it."

"It was good to see your mother last night. I haven't seen her in a long time. Not since Randy and Flora got married."

"It seems like everyone's life has pulled them in separate directions. When I was a teenager, all I used to dream about was living in a place where everyone didn't know everything about me. I got my wish, and when I did, it ended up not being so great. I took for granted how good it is to be around someone who knows you. There's no pretending."

"Were you pretending in San Francisco?"

"Don't we all pretend? Hide the things about us that might scare someone away?"

"What could you have to hide that would scare someone away?"

"That I'm afraid of scorpions. Fortunately, it wasn't something I have to worry about in San Francisco. Give me a mouse any day."

"I'm sure no one would hold that against you. You don't give the women of San Francisco much credit."

"I wasn't talking about women. I was talking about everyone."

"Oh." She looked embarrassed for a moment. "Part of me still has a hard time believing you never found anyone to marry while you were there. Every letter you sent, I thought, this will be the one where he tells me he's met someone."

He wanted to ask her how she would have felt if he did, but he refrained. "I thought the same thing. I thought you would come out of college engaged, and then when you went to graduate school, I was sure it was going to happen."

"Well, finding a husband would probably require dating, which is something I didn't do."

"You can fall in love with someone without ever going on a date."

"You think?"

"I know. It happens all the time."

They both fell quiet for a moment, probably afraid to continue the conversation. They ate breakfast together and then watched some television. *Soul Train* was on, but he didn't remember much after that, because he fell asleep on her couch.

He woke up to the sound of running water. He looked over to see Billie at the sink, washing dishes. She hummed softly. He was content to watch her for a few minutes. It was peaceful. The anxious sensation that had settled in his chest that morning had floated away. He didn't want to lose this new feeling.

She shut the water off and turned to look at him as if she could feel his eyes on her. She smiled softly at him. "Hello, sleeping beauty. You've been out cold for hours. Didn't even stir when I started to vacuum."

He sat up. "I didn't mean to fall asleep. I hope I didn't keep you from your plans today. You could have kicked me out."

"I had no plans, but if you're going to hang out here today, you have to go say hello to my parents."

"Let's go say hello then."

They went into the main part of the house. It hadn't changed much since the last time he was there except for the new avocado-green linoleum in the kitchen. He had spent so much of his childhood here, it was like a second home to him. They chatted with Billie's parents for a while, and then Wyatt ended up playing a few rounds of chess with William.

Billie helped her mother cook dinner. They made a ham and noodle casserole, which was one of his favorite dishes that Mrs. Keenan made when he was a kid.

It was an entirely relaxing day, which ended with them eating bowls of vanilla ice cream. The Keenans lived on a quiet street, so when there was a sudden banging noise, they all heard it as clearly as if it had come from inside the house.

Wyatt stood up immediately and headed toward the front door.

"It's probably just an animal that got into a garbage can," Mrs. Keenan said.

"That would have to be a very large animal, Deb," her husband replied.

When they heard a series of loud pops, Wyatt knew there was no animal.

Firecrackers. It was unmistakable. He could just make out some figures at the end of the block. He took off in that direction.

"Wyatt, are you insane?" he heard Billie yell. He ignored her. These kids were running wild around town. People worked too hard for what they had to have some bored kids destroy their property. He was almost on them before they noticed him. There was already one destroyed mailbox that he passed at the very end of the block. It belonged to a house that was up for sale. They were escalating. Fireworks could be dangerous. It was only a matter of time before someone got hurt.

He heard one of the boys call a warning to the others, and they scattered. There were three of them. He grabbed the collar of the boy closest to him.

The kid yelled for help, but his friends were running away as fast as their legs could take them.

"Get off me!"

Wyatt finally got a good look at the boy. He had one of those David Cassidy haircuts and couldn't have been more than thirteen or fourteen. Renee and Donald had been right.

"Wyatt." Billie ran up to him, out of breath. "You're fast and in way better shape than I am." She rested her hands on her knees and caught her breath.

Despite his anger with the kid, he found her adorable. "What are you doing following me? You didn't know who was down here. It could have been dangerous."

"I came to help you. I couldn't stay at the house and let you get beat up."

"I think I'm safe from that." He looked at the kid again. The boy was terrified. The neighbors must have heard the commotion, because they started coming out of their houses.

Billie's parents pulled up in their car. William rolled down the window and looked at Wyatt's captive. "You're Ingrid Severson's boy, aren't you?"

The kid's eyes went wide. "No."

"Your father's name is Mike. He works for the electric company. Your mother runs one of the gift shops in town. Your name is Kenny."

"How do you know all that?" the kid asked.

"I'm a pharmacist at the drugstore. I know a little bit about everyone." He looked back at Wyatt. "Put him in the car. We'll have his parents pick him up."

"No. Don't call them! I'll never see the light of day again."

"So you're suggesting that we just let you go?" Billie asked incredulously.

"I promise I won't do it again."

"What about your friends? You all did this together."

Wyatt squeezed the boy's shoulder. "We can call your parents, or we can go down to the marshal's office and they can call your parents. Either way, you aren't getting away with this. But it's up to you if we get law enforcement involved."

Kenny seemed to deflate. They all got in the car with Billie's parents and took him to the house.

After Billie's parents and Kenny went into the house, Wyatt looked over at Billie, who seemed to have recovered from her run.

"While I appreciate you having my back, next time stay in the house. Anything could have happened."

"While I would like to promise that, I can't."

He poked her in the side. "Why do you have to be so difficult?"

"Because if you're going down, I'm going with you!"

He cupped her face in his hands and kissed her forehead. He was in serious trouble when it came to her. "Let's go inside. We've got an investigation to complete."

It took less than fifteen minutes for Kenny's parents to arrive. After seeing the massive size of Kenny's father paired with the thunderous look on his face, Billie didn't blame him for not wanting to get his parents involved.

"I can't believe my own son is the one who's been destroying people's property. We raised you better than this!" his father yelled. "I was just talking about this at work today. Do you know how embarrassing it's going to be to show my face there now?"

"It wasn't just him," Wyatt interjected. "There were two other boys with him, but I could only catch one, and Kenny was it."

"Who were the other boys?" Mike asked his son. Kenny stayed quiet. He looked scared, but it didn't look like he was about to give up his friends. "You tell me right now, or you won't be able to leave the house without an adult escort till you're eighteen."

"I know who it is, Mike," Kenny's mother, Ingrid, said with a sigh. "Pete Jensen and Sam Jones. They've come by the house to get Kenny a few times. Pete was carrying a bat. He said they were going to be hitting some balls out in the desert. I guess they were hitting mailboxes instead."

"Tonight it was firecrackers," Billie's father said. "If they had stuck to bats, we might not have heard it. The mailbox up the road is destroyed. They're lucky a spark didn't catch something. It could have been much worse."

"Why on earth would you do something like that?" Ingrid asked.

Kenny shrugged. "I don't know. We were just fooling around. We weren't trying to hurt anyone."

"Well, you're going to pay for that mailbox and whatever other property you've destroyed." Mike looked at Billie's dad. "Do you know who owns the house up the road? I want him to apologize to the owner."

"That house had been up for sale for some time now. I do know some of the other owners who have had property damage though. One of them is an elderly woman who attends our church. She could use some help around the house. I think it might be a good idea if Kenny and his friends paid their debt through hard work."

"That's a great idea. Too bad there's no snow here to shovel. I feel like going back to Illinois just so he would have the pleasure of that particular chore."

"Were you the ones who threw the rock through our window?" Billie asked. "There's been some weird things going on at the restaurant, and we need them to stop."

"Rocks?" Kenny shook his head. "We haven't thrown any rocks."

"When did this happen?" Ingrid asked.

"It was a few weeks ago," Wyatt said. "It happened around ten in the morning."

"Was it a weekday?" Ingrid asked.

"Yes. I believe it was a Wednesday," Billie answered.

"Not that I would put it past Kenny and his crew to do something like that, but Kenny attends the summer program at his school. I signed him up to stay out of trouble, but apparently it doesn't stop his evening activities."

"Sam and Pete go to the program with me, so it wasn't them either."

It would have been so convenient for it to be the kids who had been causing trouble at the restaurant, but Billie believed Kenny's story.

"They do go to the program with him," Ingrid confirmed. "That's how they got so close this summer. I'll confirm with the school that all three were there the day your window got broken."

"We're also going to call the boys' parents tonight," Mike told them. "The vandalism will stop. I promise you that." He looked at his son. "Go get in the car."

Kenny stood up, his gaze locked on the floor. "I'm sorry for everything," he said before he went out the door.

Kenny's father shook Wyatt's hand. "Let me know when your restaurant opens. I'll send Kenny down there to work for you. You can make him scrub the bathroom for all I care. He needs to make up for what he did."

"Thank you, Mike," Wyatt said.

"No, thank *you* for catching him. We wouldn't have had any idea. They could have gotten in much more serious trouble if you hadn't done what you did."

"Don't mention it."

They said their goodbyes and left. Wyatt sank down on the couch and closed his eyes. "They didn't break the window. Which means they probably didn't open the back door and shut off the power."

"Those could all just be coincidences," Billie said, not even believing herself.

"Are there problems at the restaurant?" her father asked.

"Not really. Just minor hiccups here and there."

"I still think the range was broken by accident," Billie said.

She knew Wyatt never believed that, but she couldn't see why someone would try to cut the cord. But she also couldn't see why anyone would throw a rock through the window.

"It wouldn't be life if a few things didn't come along to ruin your day," her father said. "When we built the in-law apartment, everything that could go wrong did go wrong. Right, Deb?"

"Don't remind me." She shuddered. "We lived with a giant hole in the side of the house for months. The only thing shielding us from the elements was a thick sheet of plastic. You don't know how many times I wanted to shake the living daylights out of you."

"I think it made our marriage stronger." He grinned at her.

Wyatt stood up. "You're right. It's foolish of me to think everything should go smoothly. I've been bothering you all day. I probably better head out."

"You weren't bothering us!" Mrs. Keenan looked offended. "You're family."

"I know." Wyatt went to hug her. "This was my second home growing up."

"It doesn't have to stop being your second home just because you're grown."

"Thank you. I appreciate that."

Billie thought she could hear a little sadness in his voice. She hated that he was rather at odds with his uncle. She was annoyed that the man couldn't even offer a little bit of his support for the restaurant.

"Mr. Keenan." Wyatt shook his head. "William. It was fun beating you at chess today. We'll have to do it again sometime."

"You only beat me once." He reached to shake Wyatt's hand. "I'll break out a deck of cards next time. See if you can beat me in gin rummy."

"I'll walk you out, Wyatt," Billie said, opening the door. His car was parked on the other side of the house at her private entrance.

"You don't have to walk me all the way," he said once they were outside. He looked down at her. It was fully dark now. The only light came from the moon and the glow from the windows. He was quite handsome in the moonlight. But then again, he was quite handsome all the time. "You sure I didn't mess up any plans you had today?"

She grabbed his hand, slipping her fingers through his. "Do you for one moment think that I wouldn't have kicked you out if you were bothering me? I'm not the type to spare your feelings."

"I guess not." He squeezed her hand. "What are you doing tomorrow?"

"Going to church. Then out for pancakes."

"I really love pancakes."

She grinned at him. "Mom likes to be there by eight thirty so she can socialize with her friends. If you don't want to ride with us, be there a little before nine."

"I'll be here at eight fifteen." He stroked his thumb along hers, and her stomach started feeling funny again. Fluttery and jumpy. It wasn't the first time she had felt this way when she was with him, and she knew it wouldn't be the last. This had been happening to her for years, and she'd foolishly thought it would stop over time, but the more she was with him, the stronger the feelings grew.

"Good night, Wyatt."

"Good night, Billie."

They went their separate ways, and Billie went back inside. Her father had left the room, and her mother was sitting on the couch.

"Wyatt is a good man, Billie," she said.

"Yes, Mom. I know."

"The way he looks at you…"

"How does he look at me?" she asked. She thought she felt it, but her mind might be playing tricks on her. It could be her schoolgirl crush running wild.

"He looks at you like you're the sun and his world revolves around you."

Billie felt dangerously close to crying. "He hasn't said anything to me."

"Some men have a hard time saying things like that. Others have a hard time figuring out what they're feeling. It took your brother almost losing Flora to make him realize he loved her."

"Wyatt doesn't love me," she said. "Not like that, at least."

"Oh, Billie." Her mother got up and wrapped her in a hug. "There's nothing about you he couldn't love."

CHAPTER SIX

I can do all this through him who gives me strength.
—Philippians 4:13

Wyatt walked into the office of the Rusty Spur that Monday to find Billie on the phone, a deep frown on her face. Curls sprang out of her bun that he guessed had been neat at one point. There were two pencils stuck in there, probably forgotten as she got sidetracked from whatever list she was making. She was normally the positive one, the one who soothed his anxiety about the dozens of things they were juggling before the opening. He must have been in a deep sleep this morning, because usually he heard her moving around while he got ready. She was supposed to meet him there every morning at nine, but every day she got there earlier and earlier.

In reality, this was his restaurant. He was the owner, but he couldn't think of it just as his own. She had put in as much work as he had if not more. She cared. He didn't know why she cared, but she cared deeply.

He walked up behind her and placed his hands on her shoulders. She was incredibly tense. "How can you just cancel on us the day the job was supposed to start? We had an agreement. This is a time-sensitive project." She paused. "The end of October? There's no way that's acceptable."

She hung up the phone with more force than he had expected to come from her. She was fuming. He was almost afraid to ask her what happened. He squeezed her shoulders.

"He has another job that's taking precedence over ours," she explained. "That was actually the third time I've called him today. Before, he said he wouldn't be free for another three months. This time he was willing to come in at the end of October and give us a discount on the work. But a discount isn't going to help us when we need the work done now."

"Relax, Billie. We'll find someone else."

"Don't tell me to relax! I've been on the phone all morning. No one can do the work. Everyone is magically busy when we need them the most." She turned to face him. "I shouldn't be yelling at you. I'm not mad at you. I'm just mad and need to yell."

"Yell for the both of us," he said calmly. He knew this was bad. They needed this contractor to complete the woodwork. The old-style saloon doors that were going to close off the party room from the rest of the restaurant, the waiting area in the front, the counter that needed to be sanded and refinished, and a half dozen other small jobs.

"You take a break. I'll call around. It's probably going to cost a fortune, but I'll see if I can find someone who's willing to come from a little farther out."

"I can't believe that everyone local is all booked up. There must be some handy people in town. I know there's a shop teacher at the high school. Maybe he can help." She stood up. "I'll take a trip to the hardware store. They've got to know someone who can help us."

"Let me figure this one out, Billie. You've done too much already."

"You know me, Wyatt. I can't leave a problem unsolved. I'll sit and spin all day. You need to focus on the food ordering anyway. Oh, and the mock-up of the menu is being delivered today. You need to approve it so we can send it to the printer." And with that she left.

She was a whirlwind. He was starting to believe there was nothing that could hold her back when she put her mind to it. He knew he should be more worried about this contractor bailing on them. The vision he had for the restaurant depended on getting that work done, but he also trusted Billie to take care of it. He tried to think about what life would be like when she moved away from here. Could he find someone like her? Someone that he trusted. Someone as smart and sweet and funny. He knew the answer already. He needed to stop thinking about it. It depressed him.

He sat down to complete his ordering. He was using a few different vendors, including some of the same ones his uncle used when he ran the restaurant. Most of them had been very happy to hear from him when he reached out. It made him feel good about taking all of this on.

He left the office after an hour or so to go into the main dining room. Most of the tables and chairs had arrived. The replica wagon had been delivered. It was coming together. It was coming together when at first the tasks had seemed so endless.

The door opened. He expected Billie, but his uncle came in instead.

"Hey, Uncle John." They hadn't spoken much in the past few weeks. He was surprised to see him, especially here.

"Hi, son." He looked around. "I just came to see how things were going in here."

"They're going. It's coming together."

"It looks very different. I almost don't recognize the place. It's more upscale than I thought."

"We still aren't done, but I don't think it's too fancy. I want this to be a place where people can relax and have a good time but also give them a little something different than they are used to." He also wanted to add that everything had to be different because his uncle had gotten rid of everything that had made this place the Rusty Spur, but he didn't say that. He didn't want to argue.

Uncle John nodded. "Your mother raved about the food from the menu tasting. She said that you've got a kid cooking."

"I do. He's only nineteen, but he cooked in his uncle's restaurant before he moved here. I thought we had a lot in common, so I gave him a shot."

"Nineteen is so young. Are you sure he's up for it?"

"He is for now. If he wants to move on later or go to school, he has my blessing. He's a good kid. I had ideas, but he took them to another level. He's a talented cook. If he wants to go to culinary school one day, I'll consider helping him."

"Your aunt was annoyed that we missed out. Your mother hasn't stopped talking about the steak dish."

He nodded with pride. "It's a smothered steak with onions and mashed potatoes, but it's the gravy that makes it special. I've actually got some in the back. Donald has been in here tweaking some things and showing the other cooks the recipes. You want to try some of it?"

"I would, if you don't mind."

"You're my uncle. Why would I mind?"

He followed him to the kitchen, where Wyatt heated up the left-over food. They took it to the office, which also was a surreal moment for him. He was so used to seeing his uncle behind the desk. Now he was the one there.

Uncle John eyed the desk. "I've never seen so many papers on this desk. I see you're ordering supplies. Are you're using the same vendors I did?"

"A lot of them are the same. I'm going with a different meat guy."

His eyes settled on the calendar behind Wyatt. "You've got everything all planned out. I don't think I've ever been that organized in my life."

"That's mostly Billie's doing. She loves to make a plan. The neat piles are hers. The mess is mine. I'm going to have to clean up before she gets back."

"I hear that Billie's been like a tornado. She's been all over town getting things done. Who knew she had it in her? She was such a sweet, quiet kid when she worked here."

"She's picked up some experience working while she was in grad school. I'm waiting for her to tell me which job offer she's going to take. She's staying through opening and promised to train a replacement before she goes. But honestly, no one will be able to do what she can."

"You can hire a bookkeeper after she leaves. The hardest work you two will be doing is getting this place open. You can find someone else to do her job, but you're right, you won't be able to replace her."

"I don't want her to leave," he admitted.

"Does she know that?"

"Of course she doesn't. And I'm not going to tell her either."

His uncle raised a single brow at him, telling him everything he thought without saying a word.

"I have my reasons. Try the food. It's getting cold."

His uncle took a bite of the steak, and this time both of his brows went up. "There's a kick to this."

"You like it?"

"It's excellent," he said as if it pained him. "What cut of meat is it?"

"It's a cowboy cut. Or a ribeye, if you want to get technical."

"That's a pricey cut of meat. You sure you want to spend that much? Since you're smothering it, you could go with a cheaper cut. This gravy is good enough, you could put it on a shoe and make it edible."

"I could do that, but I want the customers to leave here thinking about that steak. It'll get them to come back."

"You've thought a lot about this."

"I'm serious about it."

"But you're not serious about Billie," he said, and it hit Wyatt right in the chest.

"That's complicated." He shook his head. "You wouldn't understand."

"Explain to me what I don't understand."

"We're friends. I want her to have the life she's worked hard to get."

"You two are closer than friends, and you know it."

"I don't want to talk about it." This wasn't something he could talk about with his uncle. It wasn't something he could talk about with anyone. He had come back here to radically change his life. It wasn't fair to ask Billie to radically change hers. "Are you going to cash my check for the restaurant?"

"I don't want to take your money."

"You aren't taking my money. You're selling me your half of the restaurant."

"Something doesn't feel right about it."

"You want to be a silent partner then? That's basically what I was when I inherited Dad's half."

He shook his head. "I don't know what I want."

"Well, we can't continue to be stuck in the same place."

"You're right, but I don't know what's going to change it."

Billie walked out of the general store. She was tired. Her feet hurt. She was a little sweaty, but she had accomplished what she set out to do. Tomorrow morning, a crew of the town's handiest citizens were coming to help finish the renovation of the restaurant. She thought she would have to beg, but it turned out people were eager to help them. Being back here for the past few months had made her realize how much she'd missed being home. She liked seeing her parents every day. She liked going to church with people she had known her entire life.

She liked being with Wyatt. Well, she more than liked being with Wyatt. But that was another story.

"Billie!" She heard someone call her as she walked to her car. She turned around to see Dave Michael.

"Oh, hi." She was surprised to see him in town. He usually stayed holed up at the resort.

"Did I startle you? I kept calling, but you seemed lost in thought."

"It's crunch time for us. We're opening soon. There's a lot to get done."

"Same for us." He studied her in a way that made her a little uncomfortable. She couldn't put her finger on it, but there was something about him she didn't trust.

"What are you doing in town? I'm sure you must have a lot going on up at the resort this morning."

"I was just meeting the locals, like you suggested. I hired a few contractors from the area to finish the work."

"Excuse me?" The hairs on the back of Billie's neck stood up.

"Yup. Three or four of them. It cost us a little more than I would have liked, but hey—" He laughed. "It's not my money I'm spending."

"Why did you hire local contractors now? I thought you had guys from out of state doing the work."

"I'm taking your advice. I see the value now of having locals complete the job. They'll be invested in the resort, feel like they own a little piece of it. They also know the look of the area more than outsiders would. Their finishing touches will really make the place shine."

He seemed so proud of himself. He was the reason they were scrambling to find people to help them finish the restaurant. He had to have known that one of the contractors he hired was supposed to work for them first. He had to have done this on purpose, to sabotage them. There was no other explanation.

"I need to go," Billie said. She had a few dozen other choice words she wanted to say to him, and she knew she had to leave before they slipped out.

"Wait a second. I wanted to talk to you for a reason."

"If you want to brag about hiring all the contractors in town, mission accomplished. I don't need to hear anymore."

He looked bewildered for a moment. "That's not why. I want to find out what's going on between you and Wyatt."

"I'm not sure that's any of your business."

"Well, it could be our business."

It was her turn to be bewildered. "What are you trying to say?"

"I've been asking around about you. It seems like Clark would never have gotten so far without you. You're the one making his restaurant dream happen."

"I'm not. All the ideas are his. I just help him."

"Yeah." He rolled his eyes. "You keep believing that. He doesn't appreciate you, if you ask me. I heard around town that you've got an MBA and a degree in accounting. You're smart, and you know how to make businesses function. You could work at our resort as the operations manager. We would pay you very generously, and you wouldn't have to leave Tombstone. You're a part of this community. No one wants to see you go. This could be the perfect opportunity for you."

Billie stood there, blinking for a moment. To say she was shocked was an understatement. A job offer from Dave Michael was the last thing she had expected. "I'm working with Wyatt right now."

"Yes, for now. But after he opens? What's there for you? Everyone knows you're planning to leave soon. Your promise to him will be fulfilled, and you could slide into a well-paying job."

"I can't accept your offer."

"Don't say no. Just think about it." He turned to walk away. "I'll return for your answer after the Rusty Spur opens."

Billie got into her car and drove back to the Rusty Spur. Wyatt was in the front of the house with Renee, going over the table layout, when she walked in.

"I wasn't sure if you wanted to start taking reservations," Renee said to him, motioning to the party area. "They want twenty seats for opening night. I didn't know what to tell them. Since it's people from Ms. Keenan's mother's church, I thought we might want to consider having them for the soft opening."

"That's a good idea, Renee. I wasn't prepared to start taking reservations yet anyway. Can you call them back with that offer?"

"Yes, Mr. Clark. Is there anyone else you want me to call and invite to the soft opening?"

"I think we should invite all the local business owners, but those are calls I'll make myself. You can invite your family though. I think they would get a kick out of seeing you working."

Renee's eyes went big. "Oh, no! My mother makes me nervous when she watches me. I'll drop all the food."

"Fair enough." He grinned. "Let me know what the church group says."

"Hello, Ms. Keenan," Renee said cheerfully as she walked away to make her phone call.

Billie waved as she headed toward Wyatt.

"What's wrong?" he asked her, keeping his voice low. "Do I need to do a search for contractors in other towns?"

"No, we'll have a full crew here tomorrow. They're a ragtag bunch, but I think they'll be able to get the job done. You should invite them to the soft opening as well."

"I will." He frowned at her. "Something else is wrong."

Billie felt very off after her run-in with Dave. She knew she didn't trust him, but his job offer was also enticing. He'd hit her exactly where it hurt. She didn't want to leave here again, and no matter how deep her attachment to the Rusty Spur was, it wasn't her restaurant. It was Wyatt's. What was her place after it opened?

She had other job offers, but she was pretty sure that after this summer of being so active she would be miserable sitting behind a desk looking at numbers all day. She was more confused over what to do with her life than she had been at the beginning of the summer. Life would be so much less complicated if Wyatt had never asked her to help him.

Wyatt gently lifted her chin so that her eyes met his. "Tell me."

"I ran in to Dave. He's the one who hired all the contractors in town."

He immediately stiffened. "What?"

"He said he took our advice and was trying to get the locals' support of the resort. He was proud of himself too. Chased after me to tell me what he did." She stopped. She couldn't bring herself to tell him the last, maybe most important, bit.

"What did you say to him?"

"Not much at all. I didn't want him to think he put us in a precarious position by poaching the contractors. It's better for him to think everything is fine on our end."

"I'm starting to think he's the one who's been causing all the issues we've been running into. The broken window, the power cut, the open door, the phone not working, and now the contractors... All those things were designed to slow us down but not stop us completely."

"Why would he want to slow us down? Are we really that much of a threat to him?"

"Maybe not in the long run. We'll probably take a share of his dinner customers, but I think this has more to do with when we open."

She nodded. "It's the same weekend as their opening. We'll be stealing their thunder."

"Exactly. He came here the night of the tasting to see how far along we were. That's why he asked about our furniture and suppliers. He wanted to know how else he could slow us down."

"So what do we do about it? Confront him?"

Wyatt shook his head. "We can't let him see us sweat. As far as he's concerned, everything is going perfectly for us. We'll keep our plans closely guarded and be extra vigilant when it comes to him. We only talk to people we trust."

"Okay. We'll get through this."

"Of course we will. Don't look so upset. People are already calling to make reservations. We're going to be a huge success." He wrapped his arms around her and pulled her into a comforting hug. "Don't start doubting now. You're the only thing that's keeping me going."

"I have total faith in you," she told him truthfully. What she didn't have faith in was her ability to make the right decision about her future.

ᓚᓂᓄ Chapter Seven ᓂᓄ

"Come to me, all you who are weary and burdened,
and I will give you rest."
—*Matthew 11:28*

The week of the opening had finally come. It had come too fast, and yet it seemed like they started this process years ago. They had managed to get the construction done. The crew that came out to help them were, in a word, elderly. They were mostly retired men who were either hobbyists or had held a career in the field. It might have taken a little longer to get things done, but they ended up being done so beautifully that Wyatt couldn't believe how well it turned out. It was even better than his vision.

The news about Dave hiring all the contractors had alarmed Wyatt. It put him on edge. The clues had been pointing to Dave all along, and it was the only thing that made sense. No one else would gain anything from their downfall. All week he had been extra vigilant with guarding their plans. They were so close to succeeding. He couldn't let the competition get in his way. In a few days they would open.

Today was a day off for everyone. Billie had been so efficient with her plans that she had left no loose ends to be tied. They had hired and trained the staff. The menus were in. The special guests had been invited. They were in great shape financially. He wanted everyone to rest before the opening. But he couldn't rest.

He wound up at Billie's door, and when he knocked, she opened it, seemingly not surprised to see him. "No lunch?" she asked him.

"We can go get some lunch later. I'd like for you to come with me somewhere first." He hadn't been able to stop thinking about Billie, about how this time would soon come to an end for them. It didn't sit right with him. In fact, every part of him revolted at the thought of her going to live somewhere else.

"Okay. Let me grab my purse."

"You won't need it. We aren't going very far."

She looked puzzled for a moment but closed the door behind her. They walked past his car and up the road. All the way to the end of the street where the last house was. The mailbox was still broken from when those kids put firecrackers in it.

"I've always been curious to see what the inside of this house looks like," he said to her.

"I wonder what all the neighbors' houses look like. Are you taking me to peek inside windows? You've got to get out more if that's your idea of fun, my friend."

"I do need to get out more," he said, "but we don't have to peek inside windows. I have the key for this house."

He slipped it from his pocket and opened the front door. The house smelled slightly musty from having been closed up for so long, but other than that it was in beautiful condition. He wasn't sure what made him do it, but he had called the real estate agent to ask specifically about this house last evening. He couldn't get the thought of it out of his mind.

"I remember when this house was built," she said to him. "I don't think I saw the people that lived here more than a handful of times."

This house was more modern than the one Billie's parents owned. It was a classic hacienda-style house with white stucco walls and a red clay roof. There were beautiful wood accents everywhere.

"It was a second home for them. They spent most of their year in New Jersey."

"How do you know?"

"I spoke to the Realtor." He walked through the large open living area and to the doors that led out to the covered patio. "The house is bigger than it looks from the outside. This would be a nice spot to have meals when it gets cooler."

It was a home made for a family.

"It's beautiful."

"Wait till you see the kitchen." He took her hand and led her to it. "The appliances were replaced when the owners decided to put the house on the market. They've barely been used."

He took her to see the four bedrooms and two bathrooms that remained in the house, watching her very closely to see her reaction to it all. She had been quiet, just taking everything in, not saying much. But she'd been that way the last few days. Very quiet. He wanted to blame all the work they had been putting in to make it to the opening, but he sensed it was more than that.

He had tried to ask her what was wrong a few times, but she claimed she was only tired. He knew there had to be more. In the back of his mind there was a ticking clock that was never silent. They would open soon, and that would be a relief. But then she would be done here, and losing her seemed impossible to comprehend.

He wasn't sure if she wanted to stay, but he wanted her to know that if she did stay, there could be a good life for her here.

"What do you think of the house? Be honest with me."

"It's beautiful. Why did you bring me here?"

"I can't live in the restaurant. Legally. That apartment is only supposed to be used for storage space. I'm thinking about buying this place. It's time for me to put roots down."

She looked around for a moment and then back at him. "This is a big house for just you."

"Yes. It is a big house for just me. I was wondering if I might be able to find someone who would want to live in it with me."

Her eyes went wide. "You want a roommate?"

He shrugged. "A roommate could be nice, but it would have to be a very understanding roommate. One that wouldn't mind having my family come to visit. Or even your family coming to visit. They're right down the road. Do you think your parents would be good neighbors?"

"I'm almost positive that they would knock before they walked in. It's still a lot of bedrooms. What would you do with all this room?"

"I could use one room for a guest room, but in the end, I guess I would see what my roommate wanted to do. It would be her house as much as my house."

"Her?" She raised an eyebrow.

Oops. Wyatt hadn't meant to say that. He blushed. "This could be a perfect house for a wife and family," he said quietly. "I don't have that right now. I would like to someday. But I also don't have to have this house, and I don't have to make a decision right now. These are just options. It never hurts to know what could be waiting for you right in your own backyard."

"Options," she said, nodding. "It's nice to have them."

"Good. Now let's go get some lunch."

They were two short days away from opening. Billie's job was basically complete. There were no plans for her to execute. No logistics for her to figure out. Everything else was on Wyatt's shoulders. He had grown up in the restaurant business, and as she watched him train the staff this past week she knew he would have no problem running the place. He was a natural leader. She was proud of him.

He had taken her to see that house right down the block from her parents' house. It was more beautiful than she could have ever imagined. She didn't want to jump to conclusions, but her foolish heart had already taken the leap.

She had been offered the job in Phoenix. The state job with the good benefits and the pension plan. The one that would give her a respectable career and not take her far from her family. She could also go work in New York, be right in the heart of the financial district. It was the kind of opportunity she'd dreamed of when she worked her way through graduate school. It had taken her a long time to complete her degree because she had to work full-time to pay for it. Before Wyatt called her, she was so set in her plans. Get a big job. Start a new life.

But he called. And she got to spend every day with him. She got to fall in love with this town and the people who lived here all over again. But if she stayed here, it seemed like all that time and all that money would go to waste. She wanted to achieve her dreams. She just hadn't thought her dreams would change so quickly.

She left the office and headed to the kitchen, where the cooks were unloading the food the suppliers had delivered. The meat was the last to arrive. There was more chicken being packed in the walk-in refrigerator than she had seen in her entire life, but she knew that it might not be enough to get them through the next five days. There were so many people scheduled for the night of the soft opening that she wasn't sure if they could still call it soft.

It was the end of summer. There were more tourists in town getting in those last-minute summer vacations. The resort, which they finally learned the name of, The Prickly Pear, was opening. Dave had been right to keep the locals away from it. It created an air of mystery for so long that when people finally got to see it, there was a buzz of excitement. The entire town was talking about it. Their official opening wasn't until Saturday, but slowly guests had started to arrive. She had heard that many of them came from around the country to get "the cowboy experience."

"The only thing left that needs to be delivered is the produce," Donald said to Billie as he emerged from the refrigerator. "It was supposed to be here hours ago. We need to start prepping first thing in the morning." There was worry on his face, which in turn made Billie worry.

"Does Wyatt know?"

"Not yet."

"Let me call the company and see what's going on."

Donald followed her back to the office, where she called the supplier. Wyatt walked in as soon as the company picked up.

"Hello, I'm calling from the Rusty Spur to inquire about the status of our produce delivery."

A long moment passed, and then the woman on the other end of the line said, "We have that marked as delivered this morning at nine."

Billie immediately sat up straighter. "Delivered to where? We certainly didn't receive it."

"The produce wasn't delivered?" Wyatt asked, a frown settling on his face.

"The owner called last night and had the shipment delivered to the Sacred Heart Society," the supplier said. "Our driver said they were overjoyed with the delivery. They said no one had ever donated so much fresh produce."

"I see," Billie said quietly. "I'm with the owner right now. He didn't authorize for that delivery to be made. Did you get the name of the person who called?"

"What's going on, Billie?" Wyatt asked.

"We didn't get a name, ma'am. A man called identifying himself as the owner and asked us to make the switch. Are you telling me it was some kind of joke?"

A joke. A prank. A sabotage. Whatever it was, it wasn't funny.

"We still need that food delivered to the Rusty Spur," she said calmy even though she felt the panic rising. "How soon can you send out our order?"

"We'll need two days. That was an enormous order."

"We are well aware how big the order was. Our restaurant's opening is dependent on it. Please have it prepared again. It doesn't matter if the president himself calls to change the delivery. It isn't to come anywhere but here." She hung up and looked at Wyatt. "There's a problem."

"Where was the food delivered?"

"To a food pantry about half an hour from here."

"We were set up," he said with a stony expression. "We can't call and ask for the food back without looking like monsters. This was a perfectly played move." He looked at Donald. "I'm going to need you to work late tonight."

"We need to go shopping," he said, reading Wyatt's mind. "I'll round up the other cooks and get Renee to help."

"Go to every grocery store and farm stand in the area." Wyatt went over to the safe and took out some cash. "I know I'm asking a lot of you, but you know the menu better than I do. Get what you need, and come back if you run out of money."

"I won't let you down, Mr. Clark." Donald walked out with determination on his face. Billie was at a loss. She never saw this coming.

"If all the vegetables in a thirty-mile radius are mysteriously all gone, I'm going to drive up to the Grand Canyon and jump in it." Wyatt slumped into a chair.

"I didn't want to believe somebody was purposefully doing this to us, but it's obvious now these were no accidents. I can't believe someone would stoop this low."

"It's not just somebody doing this. It's Dave doing this. He can't stand that we're stealing his thunder, so he's trying to steal ours."

"That's not the only thing he's trying to steal. There was something I should have told you sooner, but I was afraid of how you would react."

"What are you talking about?" He sat up straight.

"Remember when I ran into him the other day? I didn't tell you everything he said to me."

Wyatt's eyes narrowed, and his body went stiff. "What did he say?"

"He offered me a job as his operations manager. He said you didn't appreciate me and that I could work for him. I think he was trying to get into my head."

"He did what? That's going way too far. He could burn this whole restaurant down for all I care, but there's no way he's stealing you from me. I'm going up there." Wyatt grabbed his keys off his desk and stormed out. Billie ran after him.

"Wyatt, wait! What are you going to do?"

"Confront him. I've had enough." He got in the car and started it. Billie got in just before he pulled away.

"I'm not sure this is such a good idea."

"I'm going whether you think it's a good idea or not."

Billie stopped talking. There was no use. There was nothing she could say to Wyatt to change his mind. It was a quick drive up to the Pricky Pear. Unlike the last time they were there, it wasn't empty. There were cars in the guest parking lot and a few people walking around. Wyatt parked in front of the lobby door again, ignoring the employee who came out to assist them.

He was on a mission. "We'll only be a few minutes," she said apologetically as she rushed after him.

Wyatt stomped through the lobby. The woman behind the desk started to greet him but must have seen the look on Wyatt's face and thought better of it.

"Where is Dave?" he demanded.

"Down the hall and to the left," she answered.

Billie nearly had to break out into a run to keep up. Once she caught up to him, she slipped her hand into his.

They spotted Dave ahead, talking to what looked like a guest. His eyes widened as he saw Wyatt storming toward him.

"Excuse me," he said to the man he was with. The smile on his face was strained. "Wyatt and Billie. What a pleasant surprise! Step into my office."

He opened a door farther up the hallway and ushered them in, shutting the door behind them.

Wyatt stuck his finger in Dave's face. "Where do you get off offering Billie a job? It's one thing that you do everything in your power to try to prevent us from opening on time, but it's an entirely other thing, trying to steal Billie from me."

Dave frowned and took a step back. "First of all, it's not stealing. She doesn't belong to you. She's a smart woman with an MBA, and she has every right to consider my job offer. It's no secret that she's gotten other job offers. I'm offering her the one that's closest to home. As I see it, I'm helping you out. If she takes my job, she'll stay in town. What plan do you have for her after the restaurant opens? You don't expect her to stay there and be your assistant, do you? She's too good for that."

Some of Wyatt's anger seem to deflate. He looked briefly at her with something in his eyes that she couldn't read. "I would never expect her to be my assistant. I want her to choose the path that will make her happy. Even if that means that she takes a job working for you. But I want it to be clear that I don't trust you. You can mess with my business all you want, but you better not step one inch out of line with Billie."

"Hey! I haven't done anything to your business. I'm too busy trying to get this one up and running."

"You stole our contractor!" Billie retorted. "You hired all the contractors in town, leaving us to scramble to finish the restaurant. You came up to me and bragged about it."

"I did hire all the contractors in town, but it didn't have anything to do with you."

"Then explain to me who it had to do with," she demanded.

"We lost our crew," he said sheepishly. "We underestimated the time we would need them. They had to start another job. I had to do what I had to do to get everything finished. It had nothing to do with you."

"But what about the power cutting off and the broken window and the mysteriously shut-off phone lines?" Wyatt asked.

"Those seem like unfortunate mishaps to me."

"They weren't mishaps. They were done deliberately to slow down our opening so that we wouldn't compete with you. Today was the last straw. You called our supplier and told them to send my produce shipment to a food pantry instead of to us. That's costing me a fortune to replace. You're going to pay me back!"

"I did no such thing! I don't want to slow you down. In fact, I want to see how well you do, because my plan is to buy you out in a few months and make the restaurant a part of the resort."

"Why would you think I would ever sell my family restaurant to you?"

"Because it's not just your restaurant. Half of it still legally belongs to your uncle. He first approached the owner about buying the empty building. We were mildly interested, but now seeing what you've done with the place, it might be better for us to acquire it as is. You could run it for a few months and work out the kinks, and we can make you an offer later. When I spoke to your uncle the other day, he seemed to think it might take six months to a year for you to get bored. Trust me, we have no reason to see you fail. Buying your successful restaurant would only help us."

"You talked to my uncle?" Wyatt seemed dumbfounded.

"Yeah. Who do you think told me to come check out the restaurant the night you were doing the menu tasting? It looked better than our restaurant then, and I'm told that now it looks even more awesome. It'll fit perfectly with the rest of our property."

"I'm not selling you my restaurant." He turned away. "Not now. Not in six months."

"Never say never. Your uncle thinks that being an attorney is a better career for you. We could offer you a job here as well. I've done my research on you, Clark. You were good at what you did."

Wyatt didn't look back as they left. Billie didn't know what to say to him. But it was clear to her that the person who was Wyatt's biggest obstacle was the man who was supposed to love him the most.

Wyatt drove to the Rusty Spur in silence. There were too many things going through his head to make sense of any of them. He couldn't believe it was his uncle. There had been clues pointing in that direction the entire time. But he couldn't see them. Maybe he didn't want to see them.

How could his own uncle be this much against him?

He understood Uncle John not wanting him to give up his career, but to actively participate in his downfall? It felt like a betrayal.

Wyatt still didn't want to believe it was him. He didn't want to trust Dave's word. But what else was he supposed to think?

How could he look at his uncle the same way again? The man was his second father. He had helped raise him.

He couldn't be the one to do this to him.

When he pulled back into the parking lot, Billie grabbed his hand and held it in her lap, stroking her soft fingers across his palm.

"Talk to me."

He took a deep breath. Talking seemed too hard at the moment. "I want you to know that I'll not only support your career decisions but will be happy for you in whatever path you choose," he said to her after a moment.

"I'm not going to work for Dave, if that's what you're worried about."

"I wasn't worried about it. He was right to want you."

"I've been thinking about my career, and I've come to a decision."

"What's that?"

"I'm going to take everything I've learned from this experience, build a restaurant next door to yours, and run you out of business." Even when he was feeling his worst, she never failed to make him laugh. "Your uncle totally underestimated you. A broken window and some missing produce is nothing. I'd hit you where it really hurts."

"How?"

"Scorpion infestation."

"That would do it. I'd have to throw the whole restaurant away."

She smiled softly at him and then fell quiet for a moment.

"You actually think my uncle was behind all this? Logically, it makes sense. But I just can't wrap my head around it."

"I wish I knew the right thing to say to you. God has a plan for you. I believe in that plan, and I believe in you, Wyatt. I always have and always will."

That was why he loved her. He had always loved her. He had been denying it to himself for so long, but it was the biggest reason he'd come home. For the chance to be near her.

He leaned over and kissed her cheek. "We're almost there. Let's see what's going on with this produce. We have a restaurant to open."

CHAPTER EIGHT

Above all, love each other deeply, because
love covers over a multitude of sins.
—1 Peter 4:8

To everyone else who came into contact with Wyatt that afternoon, he seemed fine. Under Donald's lead, the cooks split up and managed to get enough produce to cover the restaurant until the supplier could send them their new order. Wyatt went about his duties and even made jokes with the staff like nothing had happened. He didn't say one word about his uncle. Not even to Billie. She asked him about it a couple of times, but he always brushed off the topic, claiming that he was too busy getting the Rusty Spur open to think about it. They were busy, and a big part of her knew that Wyatt wanted to prove to his uncle that he could open the restaurant despite everything.

She also knew that even after everything that happened, Wyatt still deeply respected his uncle. There would be no angry confrontation. Wyatt would turn the other cheek and prove the man wrong by quietly displaying his excellence.

But it bothered Billie. Wyatt was kind and thoughtful and giving. He was what every man should be.

She didn't return to her parents' house after she left the restaurant that evening. Instead, she went to the Clarks' house. Wyatt's aunt Sarah wasn't home. Billie knew that she was attending Bible study this evening with Wyatt's mother. It took a few moments for him to open the door after she knocked, but when he did, he smiled when he saw her.

"Billie, what a pleasant surprise." She didn't return his smile.

"Unfortunately, I'm not here for a social call, and Wyatt would probably be very upset if he knew I was here. But I have to say this to you because I'm afraid he never will."

Uncle John shifted his feet. He broke eye contact with her and looked over her shoulder. "What's going on?"

"How long were you going to pretend that you weren't actively sabotaging your nephew?"

"Excuse me?"

"We know it was you. Well, I know it was you. I think Wyatt is still doubting it, even though everything points to you. I've been thinking about it. It could only be you. No one else would have been able to get into that back door. You were the only one with a key. You are also strong enough to move the oven and mess with the cord. You cut off the lights so you would have time to get away that night. You must have parked your car on the far side of the restaurant, where you knew we wouldn't be able to see you from any of the windows."

"Billie, I—"

"I have to give it to you. Everything could have seemed like bad luck, but the reason I know it was you was that you were in the office the day Wyatt ordered the food. You saw the vendor lists on the desk. You saw the day Wyatt had the food scheduled for delivery, and you called the company, saying you were the owner. It wasn't a lie. You technically do own the restaurant. It makes perfect sense now. It should have occurred to me this morning that the supplier wouldn't have changed the order without some kind of identifying information from you. Information that only you and Wyatt and I would know. I think Wyatt is still hoping that it wasn't you. No one wants to believe their own family would betray them."

"Betray?" He seemed shocked by her words.

"You betrayed Wyatt. You betrayed his trust. You betrayed him by being disloyal. I'm not sure how you can look yourself in the mirror."

"Come on, Billie. It was some missing produce and a broken window and the oven that I originally paid for. It wasn't all that serious."

"But it was that serious! This is Wyatt's dream. To continue the family legacy. To be like you. After his father passed, you became the most important man in his life, and you turned around and purposely tried to hurt him."

"I just wanted him to get frustrated with the process and realize that the restaurant business isn't for him."

"What's for him then? To stay in a job he doesn't like, hundreds of miles away, just so you can boast to your friends that he's an attorney? It's selfish. And if you weren't so busy being at odds with him over the restaurant, you would see how much happier he is now that he's back home. You would see how much he loves being part of a community. People love him, Uncle John. Everyone wants him to succeed. Everyone except you. You didn't have to agree with his decision to leave his career, but if you ever talked to him about his vision, saw how his face lights up when he talks about it, you would know that Wyatt is doing what's best for him."

"How did you find out it was me?"

"Dave has a big mouth. If you're going to sell a place from under a man, next time don't team up with someone who likes to talk too much." She turned to leave.

"Wait, Billie. Is Wyatt so mad that he can't forgive me?"

"He's too hurt to be mad, and the sad thing is, I don't think he'll ever tell you how badly you broke his trust."

"I love him. How can I make it up to him?"

"You can pay him back for the produce. You can also make a donation to the food pantry of fresh produce every month. Oh, and you can attend the men's Bible study group at church."

"Bible study? How is that going to make things right with Wyatt?"

"This isn't just about Wyatt. You need to make your heart right too." With that, she left. She wasn't sure how Wyatt would respond to her going there, but his uncle needed to know the impact of what he'd done.

Wyatt sat in his office after the dinner rush ended on opening night. It was the first quiet moment he'd had to himself all evening. He had never seen so many people in the Rusty Spur.

The soft opening had gone off without a hitch last night. They had done a full dinner service to a packed house filled with people from the community who helped them along the way. It truly felt like he was home again. All his major memories revolved around this place. Even if it crashed and burned in six months, he would have no regrets. But he had a feeling this was where he would be spending the rest of his life. The Rusty Spur was the biggest restaurant in town, yet the environment felt warm and intimate. They had somehow managed to create a rustic Old West-themed restaurant with a touch of elegance that was different from the other restaurants in the area.

People were excited to eat here. They were booked solid for lunch and dinner for the next week. Despite everything, they were going to be a success. There was a knock on the door, and Wyatt looked up, thinking it was Billie or Donald coming to say good night. But it was another person—one he hadn't expected to see here.

"You planning on breaking some more windows?" Wyatt asked. He didn't bother to stand. He didn't see the point.

"I only wanted to crack the window," Uncle John admitted. "My arm is still pretty good. I haven't lost my pitching skills from high school."

"If your goal was to get more money by selling the restaurant, you could have just told me that. I would have given what you asked for it. I know you think me quitting my job was a mistake, but I've invested well. I could have given you what you wanted."

"It wasn't about the money." He sat down across from Wyatt. "I don't think you understand how much your father and I wanted you to do something special with your life. Your grandfather planned our future for us. We were to take over the restaurant and run it just like he did, just like your grandfather and his father did before him. We grew up our whole lives knowing we didn't have a choice. We couldn't leave Tombstone. We were stuck here, and we swore when we had children that they weren't going to live our life. We weren't going to make them be chained to a restaurant and sacrifice every weekend and holiday to run a business. We wanted you to have a life. To see the world. And when your father passed, it became my job to make sure you got out."

"I did get out. I've seen all the world I care to see. I want to be home. My choice was to be here. I don't care what your reason was, you don't get to take my choices away from me. I understand you want to be done with this place, but it would have been nice to have been able to share this with you. But instead you decided to make things more difficult for me."

"Looking back on it, what I did does seem kind of deranged. But I really was doing what I thought was best for you at the time. Billie gave me a lot to think about."

"Billie?"

"She came to see me. Ripped me to shreds and rightfully so. I don't think I would have realized how much I betrayed your trust until she pointed it out. Telling you I'm sorry seems pointless. I don't know how or if I can regain your trust, but I promise you that I won't interfere with your life anymore."

"I appreciate that."

"Well, I won't interfere with your life after one more piece of advice. If you let Billie get away, you'd be a fool. She'd do anything for you. It's rare to have that. She's the kind of woman a man would turn the world upside down to keep happy."

"I know." She was his backbone. He'd crumble without her.

"You'll be happy to know I deposited your check. You are now the sole owner of the business. I know you don't need my support, but you have it. You're a success. I'm proud of you. I always have been, and I should have allowed you to travel your own path without my interference."

"Thank you, Uncle John."

"I know you're booked solid, but if you can squeeze in a reservation for three in the next week, I would appreciate it. And I'm going to pay just like any other customer."

"You got it. I might even charge you double to make you feel better."

Uncle John smiled at him and walked out the door. Billie walked in a few moments later. "Is the coast clear?"

This time he stood up and walked over to her, not stopping until she was wrapped in his arms.

"You didn't tell me you went to see my uncle."

"That's because it was none of your business. If he messes with you, he's going to have to deal with me."

Wyatt laughed. "I love you, Billie."

"I love you too."

"No, I really love you. I'm in love with you. Practically obsessed with you. I've loved you my whole life."

"Ditto." She grinned up at him.

"I want to spend my life with you. I want to marry you. Do you understand that?"

"I've suspected it for a little while. Why didn't you tell me sooner? It would have made my life a lot easier."

He had wanted to tell her. He must have looked at her a hundred times this summer and wanted to blurt it out. But he'd always stopped himself.

"I knew you wanted to start your career, and I didn't want to stand in the way of that. I've been avoiding the topic. I kept waiting for the day you would tell me you were going away, and I didn't want to guilt you into staying. But if you do want to take a job somewhere else, we'll make it work. I'll hire a good manager. We can travel back and forth."

"We won't be doing any traveling back and forth. I don't want to be away from you."

"That's good, because I can't help but think of this restaurant as ours. I want you here beside me, but only if that's what you want. I want to make you happy, Billie. Tell me what you need from me, and I'll make it happen."

"I want to be your wife by Christmas. I want to buy the house on the same street where I grew up. I want us to have three or four children. I want to spend my life loving you."

"That's all?"

"That's all."

He tipped her chin up and softly kissed her. She blushed and closed her eyes, and he fell in love with her all over again.

"Do you think your parents are still awake?"

"Possibly, why?"

"I would like to ask for your hand in marriage, and I don't think I can wait until morning. I would like to propose to you tonight."

"Tonight?"

"Tonight. I waited my whole life to be with you. I don't want to wait a moment longer to start our future together."

And it was a future well worth the wait.

HELD UP FOR LOVE

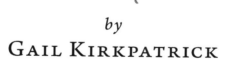

by

GAIL KIRKPATRICK

*"Accept what is, let go of what was,
and have faith in what will be."*

—Sonia Ricotti

❧ CHAPTER ONE ❧

Tombstone, Arizona
Present Day

The stagecoach bumped, dipped, and rocked over the dusty trail through the Chihuahuan Desert, much like it had over a hundred years ago when Genevieve Bowen's ancestors had moved from Rhode Island to Tombstone, Arizona. Her many-times-over great-grandparents hadn't come to mine for silver like so many others. Her great-grandfather had been a newspaperman with a craving for adventure.

Genny turned her attention away from the landscape of dirt, yucca, creosote, and mesquite to the passengers soaking up the Old West atmosphere. Wide eyes, a few leery looks, but mostly excitement, shone back at her. While this wasn't her first stagecoach ride, she still got butterflies before each journey. Unlike that of her great-grands, her journey was a one-hour trip around the Prickly Pear Resort, where she was employed.

They were halfway through the tour. They kept their groups small, and today was just five people. Two couples, one with a bored teen. The first couple was young, probably in their thirties, dressed in T-shirts and shorts, and they carried metal water bottles with them. Smart to stay hydrated. The other couple was in their late forties with the dad dressed in cargo shorts, a Hawaiian shirt, and ball cap, while his wife wore a sundress better suited to shopping in town than a dusty ride in the desert. The teen girl had on jeans—in this crazy heat!—and a T-shirt. It was Genny's job to entertain them and teach them about Tombstone's past.

"Do you know how the town got its name?" she asked the girl.

"Because people died of boredom here?"

She gave the kid a sympathetic smile. There had been a time she'd felt the same way and longed for something different. "I don't think most of the people back then had time to be bored, especially not former Army scout Ed Schieffelin. He found the first silver vein, which he estimated ran for fifty feet, and his partner named the claim Tombstone."

"Why not his name? That seems weird," the girl, Charlie, said.

"Rumor has it that when one of Schieffelin's friends found out what he was doing—searching for silver ore in the desert—he told Schieffelin the only thing he'd find was his tombstone. Maybe it became a joke between the men."

The teen shrugged, but the smirk gave her away. She wasn't as bored as she let on.

"They filed the claim with the name Tombstone, and here we are. During the busy mining years, the population grew to around ten thousand people. Within two years, it boasted four churches, a bowling alley, a school, two banks, an icehouse, and an ice cream parlor, along with three newspapers. One of which my family started."

"Your family's been here since the beginning?" Mrs. Rein, the mother of the not-really-bored teen, asked.

"They came out about a year after the town was founded. William and Mary McDaris, along with their twenty-year-old daughter, Laura Genevieve. I'm named after her."

"Did they know Doc Holliday or the Earps?" Charlie asked.

"Charlie, let her talk," Mrs. Rein said.

"It's fine. I love questions." Genny turned to Charlie. "They did. Virgil Earp was the marshal then, and he'd come by the newspaper for different things. And actually…" She hesitated for a moment to snag the girl's full attention and build suspense. Charlie's eyes were solely on Genny now. "Doc Holliday saw Laura McDaris the first day he came to Tombstone and fell instantly in love with her. He tried to court her time and time again, but her father wouldn't have it. He didn't think a dentist-turned-lawman was good enough for his daughter."

"What happened? Did they elope?" Charlie's eyes lit up with curiosity.

"No. Laura wanted to, but she didn't want to hurt her parents."

"That's sad," the other woman, Mrs. Thompson, said.

"Laura was sad for a time," said Genny. She pulled her cross and chain out from under the neck of her dress. "But her mother gave her this necklace to remind her of God's love and care for her, no matter what life brought her way."

"Did she end up marrying someone else?" Charlie asked.

"She did." Genny smiled at her. "Laura ended up marrying a man named Elias Weldon, and they had a long and happy life together." Genny let Charlie examine the small golden cross. "Through the generations, mothers have passed the necklace to daughters as a reminder of God's love and faithfulness. My mother gave it to me on my twenty-first birthday."

Charlie sighed and sat back on the hard bench.

"You said the population rose to almost ten thousand in its heyday. What is it now?" Mr. Rein asked.

"I think the last census put us around twelve hundred. Sadly, as with so many places back then, they built fast and without a thought for safety. Tombstone suffered several fires that destroyed not only a good number of the businesses but also the Grand Central Mine's hoist and pumping plant. It destroyed part of the main mine shaft as well, and then silver dropped in price."

"I'm surprised it didn't become a ghost town," Mr. Thompson said.

"We Tombstonians are made of stern stuff," Genny said.

"Whoa, whoa. That's a good horse." Hank, the driver, brought the wagon to a stop.

Worry washed through Genny. They weren't back at the resort, and they didn't normally stop in the middle of nowhere during a tour. Okay, it wasn't actually nowhere. They were still on resort property, but they were miles away from help, and the temperature sat near ninety degrees. She stuck her head out the open window.

"Hank, is everything okay?"

"Yeah, someone's coming. I'll take care of it. You all just stay inside where it's a bit cooler."

She didn't know about cooler. A bead of sweat ran down her back. Even in their summer attire, the guests looked like wilted flowers. The only one not affected by the heat was Charlie, who sat forward, presumably watching for whoever was coming. Genny had moved to exit the stagecoach when Charlie's words stopped her in her tracks.

"Is that a bandit?"

A rider on horseback approached. He wore a long, dark coat, a black cowboy hat, and a bandanna covering the bottom half of his face. *What on earth is going on?* This wasn't part of the tour package.

"Howdy, folks." The rider touched the brim of his hat. "Now, driver, you're going to want to stay right there and do as you're told." He pointed to a stand of trees where she could just make out two more men on horseback. "I know you don't want me to call my pals over there to bring a little more firepower to the situation."

"Listen here—" Hank shut up when the rider moved closer.

Had she missed a memo? No, that wasn't possible. She had her faults, but disorganized never made the list. This didn't add up. They looked like Prickly Pear Resort employees dressed in period cowboy attire. The horse even had the resort brand on his flank. But the bandanna threw her off. As the human resources assistant manager, she knew her staff, but she couldn't place his voice. As far as she could tell, the man wasn't armed, which also made sense, as they didn't allow even play guns on the property.

"You folks here a-visitin'?" The bandit edged his horse to within an arm's reach of the coach. The passengers all nodded. "Good. Good. Make sure you try a root beer float at the café before you leave. Don't nobody make a float like Miz Elizabeth. I know it's getting hot, so let's get this show on the road. In case you haven't figured it out yet, this here's a holdup."

Genny's heart beat a rapid tattoo under her hand. They didn't have holdups at the Prickly Pear. They ran a family-friendly resort.

Maybe the cowboys were confused or lost. It was extremely hot out. They might have the beginnings of heatstroke.

The passengers exchanged confused and worried looks. She flashed a playful smile, hoping to calm them while she got things under control.

"Sir." Genny moved to the window. "Hi, I'm Genevieve Bowen, the HR assistant manager. I think you have the wrong stagecoach."

"I know who you are, Miz Genny." He winked and leaned in close, dropping his voice to just above a whisper. "This is all part of the new tour package. Everything will be at the front desk when you return."

Genny bit her tongue to keep from screaming. It was so like her boss, Mac O'Neal, to leave her in the dark. It wasn't the first time, but she'd make sure it was the last. The docent should know if there was a script change. Even with Genny stepping in at the last minute because a stomach bug had hit the staff, her boss should have told her. Her priority was to accommodate the guests. She sat back in her seat and met their scared gazes.

"It's all right, folks. Everything's going to be fine. Of course, if you don't want to play along, you don't have to. If you do, we will return your 'stolen' goods once we return to the hotel."

The men chuckled as they dug out cell phones and wallets and slipped off expensive watches, dropping everything in the black loot bag. Mrs. Thompson followed suit and passed the bag to Mrs. Rein, who let out a deep sigh, her brows pinched.

"I don't think so," she said.

"That's fine, Mrs. Rein. It's all in good fun, but you don't have to participate if you don't want to." Worry clouded the woman's eyes, and it was Genny's job to set her at ease.

"Oh, come on, Mom. You're ruining everything," Charlie complained.

"All right." Mrs. Rein dropped her diamond ring, earrings, necklace, tennis bracelet, and wristlet into the bag. She passed it to their gentleman bandit. Genny expected him to ride off into the desert at that point. Instead, he turned his attention to her.

"Your turn, Miz Genny." He nodded toward her necklace.

She wrapped her fingers protectively around the gold cross.

It wasn't priceless, although she'd guess it was worth some money. It was the sentimental value. All the guests turned questioning eyes her way. Not playing along didn't look good, and the last thing she wanted to do was spoil their day. Slowly, she slipped the chain over her head then dropped it in the bag.

The gentleman bandit—because what else could she call him when he'd been so nice and polite?—touched the brim of his hat again. "Thank you much, folks. You all have a pleasant stay."

In minutes, he and his partners were gone, leaving nothing but a dust cloud in their wake. Hank got the horses moving, and they were on their way back to the hotel. Genny answered a few questions here and there, pointed out a roadrunner, and named the different desert plants for the passengers, but she couldn't settle into her groove again. Something didn't feel right.

"What do you mean, you don't know what I'm talking about?" Genny Bowen's panic-laced voice across the room reached out and grabbed Joshua Ryan-Mendoza by the heart. In all the years he'd known Genny, she'd never panicked. If she could stay calm with a rattler just feet away, then nothing could shake her. Or so he'd always believed.

He'd left Tombstone almost a decade ago with big plans. Plans that had included righting wrongs, standing up for the little guy, and having Genny at his side. But sometimes plans changed, as did people.

He excused himself from the guest he'd been talking to and moseyed over to the tour desk where Genny now talked in hushed tones. He noted the wrinkled pioneer dress, her flushed face, and that the bun holding her blond hair was askew. "What's goin' on, darlin'?"

He winked at a teen girl and her mother, staying in character. He played the role of John Henry Holliday, or, as he was better known, Doc Holliday.

Genny glanced his way before waving him off. "Not now, Doc."

"Maybe I can help?"

She took one look at him in his Old West costume and tin star and rolled her eyes. "This is not the time for a pretend sheriff. We need the real deal. Why don't you go back to flirting with the guests, Doc?"

Ouch.

Before he could respond, Nick Colangelo, the resort owner, walked up to the desk. As with all the hotel staff, Nick was in period clothing. Black slacks, pristine white long-sleeved button-down shirt, a shiny silver vest complete with a watch fob connected to a long silver chain, and an ascot tie. The total package screamed rich man in charge. Genny leaned toward the boss, whispering, "We were robbed."

Nick smiled at the crowd. "Give us a minute, folks. We'll get this all sorted out. Ms. Bowen, can you please come with me?" It wasn't just the clothes that exuded power. Nick's voice and mannerism brooked no argument. He nodded for Josh to follow.

As soon as the door shut on the manager's office, Nick told Genny to have a seat and had her run through the morning's events. Her head and shoulders drooped when she finished retelling her tale.

"I don't understand how this happened," she said. "This is a family-friendly resort. I told the guests it was okay, that it was just for fun. Now they've been robbed, and so have I."

"What did they take of yours?" Josh asked.

She looked up at him with tears shimmering in her eyes. "My cross necklace."

"Genny, I want to keep this quiet for now. If word gets out that our guests got robbed, we'll have cancellations, and I can't have that. Just leave it and the guests to me and go back to work. Or if you're too upset, take the rest of the day off." Nick stalked out of the office, leaving the two alone.

Nick hadn't revealed to Genny what Josh's actual role was at the resort, as he expected. When Nick hired him, he'd said that no one was to know that Josh was undercover. No one. He hadn't thought Nick had meant his management team. But apparently, he did. The guy didn't trust anyone.

Josh sat in the chair opposite Genny. He wanted to hug her, or at least hold her hand and remind her she wasn't in this alone. But he'd lost that privilege years ago when she broke up with him.

"Take me through the holdup again. No detail is too small or insignificant."

She sighed. "Josh, you do know that you're not really Deputy Doc Holliday, right?"

"I'm aware." If Nick hadn't kept her in the dark, it'd make this whole process smoother. "But I know how much that necklace means to you and your mom, and I'm going to do whatever I can to find it and return it to you."

Back when they were teens and he and Genny were dating, he'd heard the story of the necklace. He knew how, for over one hundred and forty years, the family passed down that necklace, from mother to daughter, on the latter's twenty-first birthday, which was Laura's age when she'd received it.

Genny and he had lain out under the stars talking about their future, making plans to leave Tombstone for college and something bigger in life. His "pie-in-the-sky dreams," she'd said. He still had big plans. They'd just changed over the years. But solving this case would help him reach those goals.

"We should call the police," Genny said.

"You heard Nick. He wants this kept quiet. If he wants the police called, he's the one to do it. Now, focus on the bandit. You said he had a bandanna covering his face. Right?"

"Yep, it was dark blue."

"Could you see his eyes? What color were they?"

She bit her thumbnail. "Maybe hazel or greenish-brown. I don't really remember. I was mad because I thought Mac O'Neal had left me out of the loop on a script change."

"Does he do that often?" Josh immediately put O'Neal on the suspect list.

"Often enough that I fell for the con." She glanced up at him. "Do you know the story of Black Bart?"

"Vaguely. Why?"

Genny chuckled and shook her head. "During the holdup, I remember mentally calling the thief a gentleman bandit. He flirted a little with me—he winked—and he wasn't armed. Not that we could see. I'm not sure about the other two, although the main guy mentioned they had 'firepower.' It just all reminded me of Black Bart, the Gentleman Bandit, except this guy didn't leave any poetry behind."

"You said that there were three bandits. Could you see their faces?" Someone hadn't done her homework well. Black Bart never made it to Arizona.

"No. They were too far away. They rode off before I could get a good look at them. We can ask Hank though. Maybe he got a better look from on top of the coach."

He could ask Hank. There would be no *we* in this investigation if he had anything to do with it.

"What else did you notice? Anything special about the horses?"

Genny's eyes sparked. "Yes, I saw the Prickly Pear brand. I'm not around the horses too often, but he could have been riding Lady Bella. She has white stockings and a long white blaze down her nose. We should go see if she's missing."

He wasn't sure where this "we" was coming from, but he needed to put a gentle stop to it right away. There was no telling what kind of people these were. If they were the same ones who had been stealing from the resort guest rooms for the past two summer seasons, they'd never resorted to violence. Until today, they'd never even confronted a guest. But Josh knew desperate people did desperate things.

"Genny, you need to go back to your office and do your job. I'll go to the barn and check out the horses."

"No, I'm coming with you."

He looked skyward as he counted to ten and prayed for patience.

"You heard Nick. He wants to keep this quiet. I can go down there and just look around. No one will think anything of it. As Doc, I wander all over the resort."

"They took my necklace. I can't imagine how devastated my mom is going to be when I tell her."

"She's going to be relieved that you're okay. Let me go there alone. I don't want to take a chance that anything will happen to you."

"That's sweet, but I'm coming with you. I'm the eyewitness and can tell you if the horse the bandit rode is there or not." She stared at him, daring him to tell her no again.

He let out a deep breath as he ran his hand over his face. He didn't know how he was going to keep his identity a secret with Genny underfoot.

Dear Lord, give me strength, and keep this stubborn woman safe.

∾ CHAPTER TWO ∾

Genny took Josh on the long route to the barn. She'd think about her reasons later. For now she told herself it was good exercise and a chance to soak up some vitamin D. She loved her job. Working her way up to management had been a goal, but she missed getting outside and mingling with the guests regularly. When Alice Wilkes, one of their seasonal docents, called in sick that morning, Genny jumped at the chance to fill in for her.

As they walked along the path that snaked around the resort to the barn, Genny wondered about the man next to her. When he'd left for college, Joshua Mendoza—he usually dropped the *Ryan*—had been a dreamer, with plans to become a big-time attorney, standing up for the ordinary guy against the corporate giants of the world. She had a million questions for him. Did he become that guy? Did he love it? Was it everything he'd imagined? And most importantly, how long was he staying in Tombstone? But fear kept her quiet.

Josh stayed in character, greeting and charming the guests with a howdy and a tip of his hat. Two little boys ran up to him. Josh knelt down to their level, answering all their questions before he produced two shiny silver badges and pinned them on the boys' shirts. He then told them it was their job to keep watch for claim jumpers and cattle rustlers. While Genny talked to the parents, she watched Josh out of the corner of her eye, noting the small physical changes.

Streaks of silver threaded throughout his dark hair. Defined cheekbones and jawline replaced the soft angles of his face. His shoulders seemed broader, his stance a little taller, but his smile… His smile was the same one that used to light up her world when directed at her.

She'd missed that smile.

"You're good with the guests," she told him.

"It's an easy gig. Smile, be nice, play along."

"The kids adore you."

"That's because I get them. I still remember playing cowboys with my brothers and sisters. Jason always played Wyatt Earp."

"And even back then, you were Doc Holliday." She stepped off the path to let a mom with a stroller pass. "How is Jason doing these days?"

"He's good. Lives in Phoenix with his wife and two girls."

A small tug pulled at her heart. She liked Josh's family, but when she broke things off, she'd distanced herself from them. If things had been different, if she hadn't backed out of their plans, she'd be an aunt. Maybe even a mom by now.

"I bet your parents make a lot of trips up north then. I can't imagine them staying away from their grandkids."

"They're living in Scottsdale. My sister's up there too."

She stopped walking as his words hit her deep inside. She'd never intended to cut the Mendoza family out of her life, just to take a breath and let the pain of missing Josh subside. "I didn't realize they'd moved. They must think I'm an awful person."

Josh took her elbow and steered her off the path so they'd have a moment of privacy. *Why would he stay in Tombstone now?* They were a vacation destination. Not exactly a booming city for lawyers or anyone else not in the tourist trade.

"They don't. Really, you're still one of their favorites. They understood we were young and life goes on." He tucked a stray strand of hair behind her ear. "Your hair has a mind of its own. I don't think it wants to be trapped in that schoolmarm bun."

"Well, there was a lot of jostling on that stagecoach this morning. I'm pretty sure Hank made it back to the resort in half the time it should have taken." She smoothed her hair, tucking strays in and thinking she should have taken a moment to fix her appearance. But then she remembered that Josh had seen her look a lot worse, like when she was seventeen and had the flu. He'd described her as looking green that day. Or any number of times they'd gone hiking. A person couldn't hike in Arizona and look fresh at the end of the day—or even five minutes after starting out.

Halfway to the barn, they ran into Ed Wilkes, one of the seasonal workers, whose wife had come down with the virus sweeping through the staff. "How's Alice feeling?" Genny asked him. "Any better?"

Ed smiled at her. "I checked on her during my morning break. She was sleeping, but her fever seems to have broken." He removed his hat to run a red handkerchief over his sweat-soaked salt-and-pepper hair. "This heat is something else, isn't it?"

"You're not used to it, I take it?" asked Josh.

"We're not." Ed put his hat back on. "We both grew up in Pittsburgh, got married, and raised our two kids there. We're not too fond of summers here, but we sure don't miss the winters!"

"Please let me know if there's anything I can do for Alice," Genny said. "I think if you stop by the café, you'll find Liz has some homemade chicken and noodles on the stove. I bet Alice would love some."

Ed thanked her, and they went on their way. For the rest of the short walk, she steered clear of talk about families. Normally, the barn teemed with people. She didn't spot a soul outside, but that wasn't surprising. The temperature had risen to near or over a hundred. Most likely, everyone was inside the air-conditioned barn.

Josh slid the barn door open. The cool air wrapped around her and pulled her in. Genny might enjoy working at a period-themed resort, but she was very thankful that she lived in the present day with all of its comforts. Josh closed the door to keep the barn cool and looked around before turning to her.

"Where are the stable hands?"

"I don't know." She poked her head into the empty barn office. Turning around, she shrugged. "They've got to be here somewhere."

"Unless they're busy absconding with their morning haul."

"Maybe." She wandered over to an empty stall. "It's too hot out for riding. Nick is very strict about the horses' care. Let me pull up the schedule and see who's supposed to be working." She walked into the barn office and tapped the computer to bring it out of sleep mode.

Boot heels thudded across the concrete floor as she went to log in. Genny left the office and walked to the stalls as one of the new employees, Shane Rodgers, came in with a hay hook in his hand. Tall, with broad shoulders and muscles built by hard work, he wore the customary cowboy attire of a dusty black T-shirt and jeans.

"If you folks are looking to book a trail ride, you'll need to come back tomorrow morning."

"Actually, we're here to talk to you," Genny said.

He squinted as he took a good look at her. "Apologies, Ms. Bowen. I didn't recognize you at first. What can I do for you today?" Shane hung up the hook and turned their way.

"Where is everyone?" she asked.

"It's just me and Colby today. Smitty's out sick, as are the other two hands. I sure hope we don't come down with this stomach bug next, because I don't know who'll fill in for us."

Neither did she. Genny had been on Nick to let Smitty hire more help for just the reason Shane stated, but he'd said no, they couldn't afford the payroll addition. She said a silent prayer, asking that Shane and Colby stay healthy.

"Please tell me Smitty has the daily chores and protocols posted somewhere along with the feed schedule?"

"He does. It's in the office."

"Good. We'll figure out something if you and Colby need help." She glanced at Josh, giving him a nod to indicate she was done.

He stood with his thumbs hooked through his belt loops and his shoulders relaxed, but his gaze scanned every inch of the barn. "Did anyone take any horses out this morning besides Hank?"

Shane hesitated before he reached for a clipboard. Just a split second. The kind of pause he'd have if he was caught with his hand in a cookie jar and his brain went into cover mode. "Not today. It's too hot."

"Any of them missing?" While Josh asked his questions, Genny walked over to a nearby stall. The two horses closest to her were both wet.

"No." Shane's gaze shifted around the barn, as if he was doing a quick head count or looking for anything that could give him away. "Why are you asking?"

"We had a report saying a couple of horses had gotten out." Not a lie. Genny had reported seeing the horses out where they shouldn't be, but she figured Josh didn't want to tip his hand if these guys were behind the holdup.

"All of the resort horses are accounted for," Shane said.

"These two are wet." Genny pointed to the two she'd looked at as she moved farther down the line. "Like they worked up a good sweat. If no one rode them, why are they wet?"

"Colby," Shane yelled.

A few moments later, Colby Summerton waltzed in, leading none other than a wet Lady Bella. Where Shane was tall, bordering on the rangy side, Colby was short with a barrel chest. Like his friend, he wore blue jeans and a dark T-shirt.

"What's up, Shane? Ma'am. Doc."

Shane nodded toward her. "Ms. Bowen and Doc are asking about the horses. If any were taken out today, or are missing, and why they're wet."

Colby led Lady Bella into her stall, taking his own sweet time. His gaze shifted to Shane and back in a blink of an eye. He scratched the side of his face, as if giving the question deep consideration. Or stalling.

"Only Hank's team went out today for the stagecoach tour. Boss Man said to keep the rest in the barn or the far pasture that's got shade. He also ordered me to give them all baths. Just finished with Lady here." He walked to the next stall and snapped the lead onto

Lightning. "Did you need anything else? I'm running behind and need to get the rest bathed before the end of shift."

His story made sense. There was a bathing station on the back side of the barn for the horses. And Nick was adamant that while the guests got a feel for the Old West, the resort—horses included— shouldn't smell like the Old West.

"Actually—" she started.

"No, we're good. We'll get out of your hair, and thanks." Josh grabbed her hand, pulled open the barn door, and tugged her outside.

As soon as they were away from the barn, out of earshot, Genny pulled her hand away. She crossed her arms, glaring. He'd forgotten how stubborn she could be when riled. He walked away, but she refused to move. *Great. Let's hope the stable hands aren't watching.*

"Why did you interrupt me?" She tapped her toes to emphasize her displeasure at him, as if he needed help. "They weren't being honest with us. I don't have proof, but they were hiding something."

"I agree, but pushing them won't get us to the truth." He didn't know either Shane or Colby, and he wasn't about to take the chance that they might do something that would put Genny in danger. "Did you recognize anything about them from this morning?"

"No. Whoever helped the Gentleman Bandit stayed hidden behind the trees. The only thing I saw of them as they rode away was their backs, through a cloud of dust."

"Come on." He glanced at the barn door. "Let's walk and talk so they don't get suspicious. What about the horses? Was it Lady Bella you saw earlier?"

Genny fell into step next to him as they walked to the resort. "If it wasn't her, it was her doppelganger. As for the other two, it's hard to say. Lady is distinctive, with the white diamond blaze and stockings, but the other two looked like typical bays. And Prickly Pear has at least three of them."

"I think it's safe to say the bandits used the resort horses. But if Shane and Colby were in on it..."

"That would explain why they're running behind on chores," Genny said.

"It does, or it could be because they're short-staffed. But if it was them, it leaves us with the question, who is the third member of their party? Only the Gentleman Bandit—wait. Why are we calling him that?"

Genny laughed. "It's silly, but it fits his demeanor. Do you have a better villain name for him? The leader of the Prickly Pear Gang, perhaps?"

"Gentleman Bandit works. Only the one spoke. Right?" They were almost back at the resort, so Josh steered them to a shady spot in the garden.

"Right, only the guy who approached the coach spoke to us, but if you're wondering if I recognized the voice, I didn't. There was a moment, when he winked at me, that I thought he seemed familiar."

"In what way?" If Genny could remember just one thing that would point him in the right direction, he might be able to finally wrap up the case he was hired to solve. But did he really want that? He'd been trying to engage her in conversation for the past week without success. Until now.

Reconnecting with Genny was half the reason he'd agreed to take the job. But as much as he wanted more time to get to know her again, solving the case and making his boss and client happy were his first priorities.

"I'm not sure. Maybe it'll come to me later." She chuckled. "Probably around two in the morning. So, what's next?"

Next? He needed a task that would keep Genny in her office. As much as he wanted her company, her safety came first. "We do our jobs. You go back to your office. I go back to playing Doc. This way, if the bandits are still on property, they'll relax."

She let out a pent-up breath. "How is that going to find my necklace and the bad guys?" Genny started to storm away, but he caught her hand, holding her in place.

"Can you access Shane's and Colby's files?"

Genny nodded.

"Find out where they worked before here. How long? Do they have references, and who? Also, who interviewed them here?"

"Smitty. He handles everything that has to do with the barn and animals. Why?"

"We'll want to talk to him when he returns to work. In the meantime, I'm going to hang out in front of Miss Maisy's Mercantile, where I can watch the barn and look like I'm doing my job as Doc."

Genny's cell phone rang. She held up a finger while she took the call. When she was done, she pocketed the phone then ran her hands over her face. He might have heard a small growl from her.

"What's up?" *Please, not another robbery.*

"Someone else calling in sick for the second shift. At this rate, the resort is going to look like a ghost town. I've got to go. As soon as I have a moment, I'll dig into those files and let you know what, if anything, I find out."

Genny's retreating form didn't match her earlier energy. Her shoulders slumped. Her steps slowed. She had probably hoped to catch the culprits in the act of returning the horses, the loot easily returnable to the guests and herself. Josh didn't blame her. But he knew from experience that cases were rarely solved with such ease or swiftness. As she disappeared inside the main building, he leaned against the post outside the mercantile where the guests could find him and interact yet he could still maintain a clear line of sight to the barn.

Shane and Colby were up to something. He had no doubt. But were they behind all the thefts? He didn't know. For the past two weeks, Josh had been reviewing security footage at night in his cabin. Not once had he seen the stable hands on the guest room floors. The operating theory from the start had been that it was an insider or, more accurately, a group of insiders. At this point, he had more questions than answers.

The stable hands started work at seven in the morning. The stagecoach holdup took place at nine thirty. So how did the bandits get the horses without the stable hands knowing or their involvement? How was it that the very day Smitty, the barn manager, who had worked at the resort for at least twenty years, called in sick, the stage was robbed? Was Smitty involved? Or one of the other stable hands that had called in sick? He also couldn't rule out Hank, the stagecoach driver, another longtime employee. But again, he hadn't seen either Smitty or Hank near the guest rooms.

He also didn't see the two old cowboys as the types who would ever do something like that. Then again, he could be wrong.

ᴄ⊙ CHAPTER THREE ⊙ᴄ

The next morning, Genny stuck a note to her computer with one word written on it: *files*. Josh's request had to wait its turn. First up, playing a round of employee-Tetris to fill in the gaps the virus left open as, one by one, the staff got sick. She was thankful that at this point most seemed to bounce back within twenty-four to forty-eight hours. Just as she finished, her door squeaked open.

"Hey, brought you something." Her lifelong best friend, Liz Hutchins, slipped into the room and set a root beer float in front of her. Like Genny, Liz had her dark brown hair up in a bun. Unlike Genny, Liz's hair was smooth and behaving itself. "You okay?"

"Of course. Why wouldn't I be?"

"Because I overheard one of the café guests talking about the coach getting held up yesterday, and you were on it."

Genny rolled her head from side to side, fighting a stress headache. "Shh, we're not supposed to talk about that. Gag order from Nick." She couldn't keep the exasperation out of her voice, and Liz's arched brows reminded Genny to tone it down.

"Okay, if we can't talk about that, let's talk about you and Josh." Liz beamed with excitement. She'd always been on #TeamJosh when it came to Genny's dates over the years.

"There's nothing to talk about." Genny glanced at the note on her computer.

"Really?" Liz slid the root beer float out of Genny's reach. "Because I heard you went off somewhere with Josh yesterday... Oh, excuse me. With Doc."

The sigh that escaped had Liz pushing the float within her reach again. "It's not like that. He's trying to figure out who was behind the holdup and get my necklace back."

Liz gasped. Her eyes got big and round. "Oh no. What are you going to tell your mom?"

"Nothing. Remember? Gag order. Although, if it's not found soon, I'll have no choice but to tell her. She'll be disappointed, but as Josh said, she'll be relieved that no one was hurt."

Liz bit down on her bottom lip. "As Josh said, huh?" The megawatt smile she flashed told Genny that her best friend hoped for a romance-book ending for the two of them. She hated to burst Liz's bubble, but she didn't see that happening.

"Stop," Genny said softly.

Liz's smile dropped, and she scooted closer, lowering her voice. "Do you think this was part of something bigger? Like, do we have an internal problem?"

"In what way?"

"Well, Nick might have you on a gag order, but the guests talk. I've heard several complaints over the summer about missing items. Electronics, jewelry, wallets, money... All missing, but I've heard nothing from Nick. Surely those people said something to the front desk. Why isn't he telling us anything?"

"I don't know, but there was something familiar about the one guy. The Gentleman Bandit knew my name, and he winked at me, like we shared some kind of secret or something."

"That's kind of weird and creepy. I'll keep my ears open at the café. See if anyone slips up or says something helpful." She pushed the float closer and smiled. "So, let's talk about you and Josh."

"We did. Remember? There's nothing to talk about." Genny took a sip of her float and let the bold, sweet flavor explode in her mouth. Just what she needed.

"Has it been hard with him being here?" Liz held up her hand as Genny started to respond. "Remember who you're talking to, Bowen. I'm the one who held your hand and ate copious amounts of ice cream with you after you broke up with him."

"Trust me, I remember. I'm incredibly lucky to call you a friend. So, truth time?" She gave a slight shake of her head as she stared at her float. *Why couldn't life be simpler?* "My elaborate plan to avoid him?"

Liz nodded.

"Hard to do when he's everywhere. He's there, opening doors for me. He's there to carry a package for me. Always with a smile and a compliment. Asks me how my day's going. How are my parents? He's caring and kind, and oh so charming. It's hard to forget our past, what I felt for him, when he's the same. All those memories, those feelings, are right there."

"Wow. You're still in love with him."

She took another sip of her float, more to give her a minute than anything. "No, I'm not. At least I don't think I am. Besides, what does it matter? He's here filling in for a friend while 'Doc Holliday' recuperates from surgery. As soon as his buddy is back to work, he'll be gone again. Back to his normal life, two thousand miles away."

"Are you sure about that?" Liz arched her brow.

"Of course. Why else would he be here? He's using his vacation time to help a friend."

"Is that what he told you?"

"No, Nick did. Why?" She spooned a bite of vanilla ice cream, unable to resist the dessert in front of her.

"Isn't it kind of a weird coincidence? We haven't seen him in years. Then he shows up a couple of weeks before the stagecoach is held up? He knows the resort, how things work, the property. Could he be behind this whole incident?"

Genny shook her head before Liz even finished. "No."

Liz's frown curled into an all-knowing smile. "Interesting."

"What?"

"You're pretty quick to defend him."

She pushed the unfinished float toward her friend, appetite gone. "It's not like that. We know him. No matter what or where he's been for the past eleven years, Joshua Mendoza is and always has been an honorable person."

"People change."

"Not Josh. He idealized his grandfather. When he didn't follow in his footsteps and join the police force, it surprised me. Although law school and defending average, ordinary people up against the corporate world is still serving people."

"You're right. I just wanted to see what you'd say, and..." Liz shrugged.

"And what?" Genny laughed as she tried to ignore that warm, jiggly feeling inside when she thought of Josh. She could not fall for him again. It had taken everything she had to break up with him—and to get over him. As it was, when 'Doc Holliday' returned to work and Josh left again, she predicted a lot of floats in her future.

"And I was—"

"Knock, knock." Josh's voice filtered through the closed door. A moment later, he poked his head into the office. His gaze landed on Liz. "Sorry. You're busy. I'll come back later."

Liz turned to her with a silly I-told-you-so grin. She mouthed "interesting" then stood.

"I need to get back to the café. See you around, Doc." She gave a little finger wave and left Genny to face her past and her future.

Josh moved deeper into Genny's office so that Liz could exit. "I didn't mean to interrupt."

"It's fine. She heard about the holdup and came to check on me." Genny glanced at her computer, her smile momentarily gone. "I haven't had a chance to look at Shane's and Colby's files, if that's what you came for."

"I came to ask you to join me for a picnic lunch." He held up a bag with the Sarsaparilla Café logo on it. "It looks like you've already had dessert."

"Life's short. Start with the best part." She hit a key on her keyboard, exhaling loudly. "I'd love to, but I have a ton of work to do."

Don't we all? And right then, he couldn't do his job without her help or breaking his cover. "I need your help, Genny."

"You do?"

"Yes. You've got knowledge and access to information that I don't. I'm trying to keep an eye on the barn, and I thought a picnic was the perfect cover for us to do that and talk where we don't have to worry about others overhearing us or wondering why we're locked up in your office for so long."

She grabbed her tablet, which clashed completely with the long blue prairie dress, and a wide-brimmed straw hat.

"Is that regulation?" He'd expected her to grab the blue ruffled bonnet that hung next to the door.

"No, but the one that is feels hot and heavy and gives my neck and shoulders no protection from the sun."

If anyone could get away with breaking the rules at the resort, it was Genny. She'd always been a favorite of the owner, which is why Josh had been surprised when Nick forbade him to tell even Genny why he was really there. He didn't believe for one minute that Nick suspected Genny of wrongdoing. There was just no way possible for her to be involved.

They sat at a picnic table under a grove of palm trees that had been planted when the resort was built. He didn't remember what the property had been used for before. Probably someone's home or ranch. While Nick originally went for the "Old West" charm almost fifty years ago, it wasn't long before he included comfort and conveniences for the guests. No muddy streets to trudge through, lots of shade and grass, two swimming pools, a kids' playground, shops where guests could load up on souvenirs, a full-service restaurant, and, of course, air conditioning in every building.

Genny placed the food he'd grabbed from the café onto the table, waving and smiling at people passing. They had a perfect view of the barn, the main building, and down Main Street.

As they dug into lunch, he nodded toward her tablet. "Okay, we need to find our third man. My gut is saying this is an inside job. If Shane and Colby aren't involved, and that's a big if, then whoever was behind the robbery knew when to access the horses, and how, without being seen."

"There's only about five stable hands, plus Smitty and Hank, who drives the stagecoach."

"Are any of them new besides Shane and Colby?"

She tapped her tablet with one hand while she held a sandwich in the other. "Well, Smitty has been here since the resort opened. Hank's been here about twenty-five years. One hand has been with us for about five years, and the other for two."

Right when the thefts started.

"This is Shane's and Colby's first year here," she added.

Could it be a ring and they alternated members each year? Shane and Colby could have worked a different target last year.

"Can you create a list of new employees for me? Also, another list of who called in sick yesterday?" He munched on a chip as he thought. It was hard to focus on the case while sitting across from Genny. He'd rather ask about her life. Was she happy here? Did she have regrets? Had she missed him?

"I can, but that second list is going to be long. There's a stomach bug going around. A good fourth of the staff is out sick, including Mac. This is his second day absent."

The last comment caught his attention. "Weird."

"What's weird?"

"I thought I saw Mac yesterday morning. He was walking into a restaurant in town. Maybe whatever is going around hit him after that." He made a mental note to look deeper into Mac O'Neal.

"Maybe. As for other new hires. Obviously, Shane and Colby and at least half of the seasonal workers, probably some of the wait staff at the café, housekeeping, maintenance, and at least two front-desk employees. That's just off the top of my head."

"Okay, we'll work our way through the list. Verify where every-one was yesterday morning during the holdup. What about the stagecoach schedule? Who can access it? Who knows the route? Oh, and who has access to costumes?"

Genny's jaw dropped open. "Wow. You're good at this. Okay... The schedule is on the website, so basically everyone in the world can see it. Anyone who has taken the tour in the last twenty years knows the route, because it hasn't changed. Or someone could watch and follow the tracks. Costumes. Anyone with a staff keycard can get into the room, which should rule out guests."

"Is there a keycard log? One that shows who used their card, when and where?"

The edges of her lips quirked up on one side. A sparkle gleamed in her eyes. "You seem to take your role as Deputy Holliday to heart. Maybe a little too much?"

Josh reached over and took her hand, giving it a reassuring squeeze. "Not to me. Look, Nick wants to keep this quiet. Even if he called in the local boys, the police don't have the manpower or any leads to follow other than letting nearby pawnshops know to be on the lookout. That's not good enough. I promised to find your necklace, and I will."

She pulled the tablet closer and started typing. "Thank you. I'll get you a list as soon as I can."

"Thanks. Can I ask you something, not dealing with the holdup?"

Genny stopped typing, and her eyes met his. "Sure."

"Why didn't you follow our plan? Join me for college?" He'd waited over a decade to ask. At first, the anger held him back, then hurt and his pride. He'd been afraid of the answer. Afraid she'd say she didn't love him, that he wasn't enough for her. Now, he simply wanted the truth.

"Bottom line, I didn't have the tuition money. I didn't qualify for enough scholarships, and I didn't want to be in debt by taking out a loan."

"And that's why you broke up with me and stayed here?"

This time, Genny took his hand and squeezed. "It wasn't you. I know that sounds like a cliché, but honestly, I was afraid, Josh. What if we broke up after I moved there? I'd be thousands of miles from home and family. What if I hated it and you loved it?"

"We'll never know, because you didn't give it a try. And I don't think we would have broken up, for the record."

Genny pushed the rest of her lunch away. "I know, and that's on me. I just kept thinking about the crazy crowds in New York City. Even during tourist season, Tombstone is nowhere like New York with millions of people, the traffic, the noise."

"It can get crazy there, that's true."

"I didn't want a life where I had to work multiple jobs to pay the rent on an apartment the size of a sardine can. And when would I have seen you? As a new lawyer, you would have been working something like ninety-plus hours a week."

"You should have told me."

She shook her head. "You loved all of that...the city, the challenges that would have come with the new job. I couldn't take that from you. Never. You were entitled to live your dream."

Josh gathered up the leftover lunch and tossed it in the nearby trash can. He needed a minute or two. She hadn't had faith in the two of them making it. But she'd also cut him loose because she wanted him to follow his dream. He didn't know if he was mad at her or himself for not seeing how she felt. For now, he'd put it aside. He had a job to do.

He sat back at the table, his eyes trained on the barn.

"Do you hate me now?" Genny whispered as unshed tears glistened.

"Never." He didn't even have to think about his response. A piece of his heart did now and always would belong to this woman. Of that, he was certain. He just didn't know if they could have a future together.

"Can I ask you a non-holdup question too?"

"Sure," he said.

"Why are you back now? Here in Tombstone?" She twisted her hands as she played with her ring.

"It's just a temporary thing, helping out a friend." Not a lie, just not the full truth. It just so happened that Nick needed a private detective at the same time his Doc Holliday needed surgery.

"I would have thought you'd be too busy practicing law in New York to take weeks off at a time." She continued to spin her ring around her finger.

"Actually, I'm living in Phoenix now, and I won't start my new job until next month." Again, it was a partial truth. He hated that he couldn't share everything with Genny. After lunch, he was going to have a talk with Nick. He needed Genny's help, and he wouldn't lie to her, but until Nick agreed, Josh was bound by his contract to keep quiet.

She stopped fidgeting, her gaze suddenly on him.

"Phoenix? That's...closer."

Hopefully, it was close enough. At least for now. He'd dated over the years, not finding anyone serious, not finding someone who could make him forget Genevieve Bowen. The transfer had come the morning after another failed date. He took it as a sign from above that it was time to revisit the past and see if there was a future. He'd only been back in Arizona for a few months. When Nick called, Josh stopped making excuses. He'd shoved the self-doubts to a dark corner of his mind, but now it was time to take the next step.

He wiped his sweaty palms on his thighs then took a drink of water to quench his dry mouth. Now or never.

"Genny, would you have dinner with me one night? Away from here. Away from the job, just two old friends reconnecting?"

ᴄ᚛ᴏ Chapter Four ᴏ᚛ᴄ

Genny stared at the man across the picnic table from her, speechless. *Go out with Josh on a date?* It was the last thing she'd expected him to ask. She'd be crazy to say yes. He'd just confirmed he was only in town temporarily, just until the guy who played Doc got back to work, which could be any day now. What would be the point? He lived in Phoenix. It was closer than New York but still a three-hour drive away. What if Liz was right about her being in love with Josh? Going out with Josh was begging to be hurt. Or maybe it wasn't. They were older, wiser. Her head said no. Her heart...

"I'd love to, Josh."

Whoa. Did that just come out of my mouth? Silly heart. It didn't remember how hard it had been last time. Or maybe it did and was trying to tell her it was time to try again. Maybe she should stop overanalyzing everything and just take a chance.

"Great. Thursday or Friday sound okay?"

Genny craned her neck to the side as she caught movement from the back of the resort. "Yeah, sure."

"That doesn't sound too enthusiastic," Josh teased.

"Josh, check that out." She pointed to the person with a large garment bag walking to the parking lot. "Come on. Let's go see."

Genny hustled across the back lawn, through the garden, and to the parking lot with Josh at her side. They reached it as the person drove off.

"What was that about?" he asked.

"Did you see her? She was in a housekeeper's uniform and carrying a large bag. What looked like a large garment bag. One that could hold three cowboy costumes in it."

"Why would a housekeeper take costumes with her? All laundry is done in-house."

"Precisely." Genny headed toward the employee entrance. "I didn't recognize her, but we were far away and, per usual, we've had a lot of new hires for the summer."

She led the way down the hall to housekeeping. They dodged around people and carts until they got to the back of the room, where they found Marta Sanchez, a wisp of a woman with a voice that could be heard three counties over.

"Genny." Marta grasped her by her upper arms as her gaze took inventory. "I heard about it this morning when I came into work. The thing on the stagecoach. Are you okay?" Her voice dropped to a whisper as if the others hadn't heard yet about the holdup.

"I am. Thank you. How did you hear about it?" She shot a look at Josh, who shrugged.

Marta waved her question off. "You know nobody sees housekeeping. Now, tell me. What can I do for you and the deputy here?"

Josh closed the door so others couldn't overhear the conversation.

"The housekeeper that just left," Josh said. "Do you know who that was?"

"Of course. Anna Jacobs. She's new, just started at the beginning of summer. She's part-time, so she only works until lunch. Why?" Marta glanced between the two of them. "You don't think she held up the stagecoach, do you? She's just a kid and so sweet. No, I can't believe that." Marta dropped into the chair behind her desk, still shaking her head.

"She was carrying what looked like a garment bag. Any idea why or what was inside?"

While Josh did his thing, Genny pulled up Anna Jacob's personnel file. *Eighteen. Tombstone native. Recent high school graduate. Plans to attend Cochise College in the fall and study art.* Genny continued to scroll down until she saw the references. Anna had listed Genny's mom, which made sense as her mom taught art at the high school. She made a mental note to ask her mom later about the girl.

Marta kept shaking her head and repeating, "I just can't believe this." Josh nudged Genny with his foot. Her turn.

"We don't know if Anna was involved in the incident or not, Marta. But given what happened, and that she was in her uniform, it seems odd that she'd have a reason to carry a garment bag to her car. Wouldn't you agree?"

"She's a good kid."

"I'm sure she is, otherwise my mom wouldn't have stood as a reference. But I still need to talk to her, if nothing else, just to clear up what she had in the bag. When does she work again?"

"Not for a couple of days. She's off until Saturday."

"Okay." Genny stood and brushed the wrinkles from her dress. "If you or your staff hear of anything else, please let us know."

"Marta seemed awfully shaken by our questions," Josh said once they were back in the hallway.

"It doesn't surprise me. She's very protective of her crew and thinks of them as family. When it's one of their birthdays, she bakes them a cake. And they all get goodies at Christmas too."

"Nice. Bet she doesn't have a high turnover rate."

"No, she doesn't, and Marta makes the other managers up their game, which is good for everyone. I have Anna Jacobs's address. We could drive over and talk to her."

"I'd rather not confront her off-site. We have no proof she took anything nor any authority to question her at home. We'll wait until her next shift."

"What's next?" She really should get back to her office or go check that all departments had adequate coverage, but she was having fun with Josh, which was so not the mission. They were trying to find a thief or thieves, as the case may be. This wasn't a date or an adventure. The man was messing with her brain, and he didn't even have a clue.

"Let's go check out the costume room and check for any missing inventory." When they got there he used his employee badge to open the door. "It's possible the three don't even work here. They could have been outsiders. The guests wouldn't have known they weren't staff. Getting the horses unseen could have been pure chance."

Genny reached for her absent necklace, missing its comforting weight. "I hope that's not the case, because I'll never get my necklace back then."

"We'll get it back. I'm trying to keep an open mind."

"And a positive attitude. That's so like you. Always the dreamer, always believing you can solve everyone's problems."

"Is that a bad thing?" They headed to the men's side, and Genny picked up the check-out sheet.

"There should be twice the number of names on this sheet. This stomach virus is sweeping through the place. Can you read off the numbers for me, and I'll compare them to the sheet?" She purposely avoided answering Josh's question because she didn't know the answer. His big plans were part of the problem eleven years ago, but she didn't know about now. She didn't know if it even mattered. Yes, he'd asked her out for dinner. It was one date. One night. Not a lifetime commitment. She needed to focus on the task at hand...finding the bandits and getting back everything they stole.

Josh pulled out an old costume that probably hadn't been worn in years. There was a ripped seam on the shirt, and the pants were frayed at the hem. "Remember this? I think it was my first uniform here."

"You made a great bellhop. Very cute with your lopsided smile that stole all the ladies' hearts and garnered you a lot of tips." She checked off the number and tried not to remember those early days.

"Bet I could find your first costume." He flashed her that lopsided grin and zipped across the room to the women's section. He flipped through clothes with a few *hmms* and a lot of nopes until he pulled out the costume that had tormented Genny for a solid summer. Denim blue, with a white petticoat and a collar that buttoned up to her nose. Hot, heavy, and constricting around her throat. At least Nick hadn't made her wear the bonnet most of the time. "You looked like Laura Ingalls in this. All the boys had a crush on you."

She laughed as she rolled her eyes at his silliness. "No they didn't."

"I did." He tucked the same rogue strand of hair behind her ear again. "You were the prettiest girl I'd ever seen."

"*Were* being the key word?" *I'm not fishing for compliments.* She repeated that over and over in her head, but a part of her was dying to hear Josh say it was still true.

"Well, I've seen more of the world now." He shrugged one shoulder and sauntered back to the men's section, his lips tilting upward. She refused to take the bait, instead focusing on checking off inventory. Five costumes in, he finally turned to her. "You're still the prettiest woman I've ever seen, and one of the nicest, Genny. The world would be a better place if there were more people like you in it."

Tears welled in her eyes. She swallowed hard, sucking in air through her nose as she willed herself not to cry. Josh's words didn't just touch her heart—they pierced it dead in the center. For years, she'd thought he hated her, and she didn't blame him one bit. His words weren't simply a compliment. They were a comfort, easing the guilt that she'd carried for years over hurting Josh.

"Thank you." She tried not to think about the fact that his words also made her feel warm and happy, almost giddy, and what that meant. "We should finish checking the inventory before people notice we've disappeared. Don't want anyone asking questions if we're supposed to keep this whole thing quiet."

Together, they finished going through the men's outfits. In the end, Genny noticed three unchecked numbers on her sheet. She brought up their descriptions on her tablet.

"Looks like you were right. It was an inside job, or they had inside help," she said.

CHAPTER FIVE

After another night of tossing and turning, Genny arrived at work earlier than usual, which was a good thing. She had over a dozen voice messages and emails from staff members calling in sick. For the next hour, she worked to fill those gaps or notify supervisors they'd be short-staffed again. One message in particular caught her attention. Smitty's wife called. He had been admitted into the hospital with pneumonia. She and Josh could cross him off their short list. Genny also made a quick note to send him a care basket when he got released.

As much as she'd rather not, which was a lot considering she'd rather have a root canal without anesthesia than talk to Mac, she knew she had to update him on the staff and the holdup. He'd probably blame her for both the virus and the robbery. No matter what she did, Mac always found her lacking. She grabbed her tablet and headed to her boss's office. His door was cracked open with the light on. *Great, he's in.* She said a brief prayer asking for strength because one of these days she was going to snap and quit. Genny couldn't quit without a plan though. She liked to eat too much.

After saying a second prayer asking for forgiveness for wishing Mac was still sick, Genny reached for the handle but hesitated when she heard him talking.

"Thanks for the other day…"

Since no one responded, she assumed he was on the phone. She could slip away and postpone the meeting. That thought had appeal. She'd just taken a step when she heard him talking again. For some reason, her gut told her to stay, even though eavesdropping was wrong. This was her boss. She might not like the man, but she should show him some respect. Except Josh had said the robbery was an inside job. Mac had the opportunity. Who's to say he wasn't involved? But what was his motive? Instead of leaving, she crept closer to the inner office door.

"Tomorrow night? Yes, I can meet with you. What time? Eight thirty at the Rusty Spur is perfect. I can wrap things up here and not worry that anyone from work will see us."

Why would Mac worry about someone from work seeing him with someone else? He wasn't married. Could he be seeing an employee? They didn't have rules against dating coworkers, but given Mac was the personnel manager, it could be construed as wrong. Who was this mystery person in Mac O'Neal's life, and what did they do for him when he was supposed to be home sick?

She'd mention the call to Josh, but for all she knew, the person could have been taking care of Mac while he was ill and now he was paying that person back with dinner. But the Rusty Spur? That was definitely out of the way. She took a deep breath, because dealing with her boss was always a challenge, and pushed the door open. Mac took one look at her and slammed his phone down.

"Haven't you heard of knocking?" A moment ago, he was nice, even cordial to the person on the phone. In the blink of an eye, he turned into a snarling beast. Maybe he was still a little under the weather? No one was at their best when they were sick.

"Sorry, the door was open. I just wanted to see how you're feeling." She tried to infuse her voice with concern, but he made her life difficult on pretty much any day that ended with a *Y*.

"I'm fine." His words were short and clipped, but at least the growl was gone. "What do you need?"

She let him know that the stomach bug was still going around. "At least twelve of our daytime staff have called in sick, and Smitty's in the hospital."

"So deal with it. That's your job, isn't it?" He turned toward his computer. "I've got work of my own to do."

"Of course." She should scurry away while she still had her head attached. *Should* being the key word there. "Did you hear about the holdup?"

"What?"

Genny filled him in on the excitement, but Mac wasn't interested.

"If Nick says he's handling it, then it's his problem, not mine. Is there anything else?"

She nodded. "Shane Rogers and Colby Summerton."

Mac glared at her. "What about them?"

"I didn't see any references in their records."

"Why are you in their records? Never mind. If you have a problem or a question regarding them, you'll need to take it up with Smitty. You know Nick gives that man full control over the stable hands. Now, I believe you said we have a staffing issue. Go fix it."

She needed fresh air.

And a place to scream where no one could hear her.

And possibly a new job.

Genny had started at the Prickly Pear Resort when she was sixteen. She'd worked summers and weekends until she graduated high school, moving her way up from waitress to front desk clerk to human resources assistant and then finally to her present role as assistant HR manager. When her former boss retired, she'd hoped that Nick would promote her to HR manager. Instead, he hired Mac, stating Genny was too young and inexperienced. That was two years ago. During that time, Mac had gone out of his way to micromanage Genny's work and undermine her. The only reason she was still there was because Nick liked her and had helped pay for her college tuition.

But what Genny really wanted was the opportunity to work her way up to hotel manager. Chances of that happening at the Prickly Pear were slim. Nick, as owner, held that role. He liked to be hands-on.

Maybe it was time for a change?

She'd give it some real thought later. Right now, she needed to talk to Liz at the café because Quincy, the piano player, called in sick, which meant no dinner entertainment.

When she stepped outside, the morning sun instantly blinded her as heat wrapped around her like a wool blanket. It was like sticking her head in an oven. Her dress stuck to her skin, and perspiration peppered her hairline. Another glorious summer day in Tombstone. Despite the oppressive heat, she loved being outside. Breathing in fresh air, blue skies overhead with fluffy white clouds, and kids and parents strolling down Main Street.

"Morning, Ms. Genny." Josh's deep, warm bass of a voice washed over her. "I brought you something."

He handed her a large to-go cup. She lifted the lid and smiled when she found it filled with iced tea, her favorite.

"Why, Deputy Holliday, how thoughtful of you." She put a little old-fashioned charm in her reply as a group of tourists walked past. Once they were out of earshot, she dropped the act. "You are a lifesaver. Thank you."

"Rough morning?"

"Every time I closed my eyes last night, I had nightmares, which is silly. The holdup couldn't have been more G-rated. Not for one second did I feel like we were in danger. So I don't know why my subconscious is turning it into something else."

"Hindsight."

"What?"

"You thought it was an act. Now you know differently, and your subconscious is playing out other scenarios of how it could have gone."

"I could do without the alternative plot lines."

"You'll feel better once we find the crooks."

They stood in front of the main building, blocking the path to the front door, so Genny started walking to the café. Josh fell into step beside her as she knew he would.

She thought about what he said and hoped he was right. "How was your evening?"

He glanced toward the barn. "I stuck around to watch the activity down by the stables. Shane and Colby did nothing out of the ordinary other than work late. Given the shortages in staff, that seems legit, but my gut is telling me there's something off there."

"You might be right. By the way, Smitty's in the hospital, so we can cross him off the list. They admitted him yesterday with pneumonia, according to his wife's message."

"Did Mac O'Neal finally make it in today?" His hand landed on the small of her back as he steered her up onto the wooden walk that ran in front of the stores and restaurants.

"Unfortunately, yes." She filled him in on the call she overheard and Mac's less-than-sunny attitude toward her. "At first, I thought nothing of it. He's always a jerk to me, but he was more so today. Like he was on the defensive. Do you think he's worried that I overheard the call?"

"Could be. How do you feel about an unconventional dinner tomorrow night?"

"Um, sure."

"Good. You said he's meeting this person at eight thirty, right?" She nodded. "Good. Be ready at seven thirty."

"Okay, but what's next? We can't talk to Smitty, and Anna is still off today. Do we have any other suspects besides Shane and Colby?"

"I need to talk to Hank."

She put her hand on Josh's arm. "Hank's not involved."

"How do you know?"

She crossed her arms and glared what she hoped was an are-you-kidding-me glare that would bring Josh to his senses. When he didn't respond, she let out a long, exaggerated sigh.

"You've got to be joking. We've known Hank since we were kids. I've worked with him for the past eleven years. He's married. He's a grandpa."

He moved in close and dropped his voice to just above a whisper. "We can't rule someone out just because they have grandkids. Or because we've known them a long time. That he had access to the costumes, the barn schedule, and not only knew the route but the best place to hold up the coach means we have to consider him."

"Fine, but if you're interviewing Hank, I'm coming with you."

She could deal with the piano and entertainment situation later.

A smart man would discourage Genny from coming along. A wise man would know not to try. Josh wasn't sure if he was smart or wise, but he didn't argue. Having her along meant risking his cover. Not that she'd tell anyone else, except for Liz. And Josh would willingly bet the bank that Liz was no more involved in the theft ring than he or Genny was.

They strolled past the main barn until they reached a carriage house used to store the stagecoach. Inside, Hank was wiping the seats.

"Howdy." He stuck his head out the open door. "What brings you two here? I thought Alice was back at work today."

"She is. We came to talk. Can you spare a few minutes, Hank?" Genny flashed him a smile that could light up the Chihuahuan Desert sky.

Hank climbed down from the coach, sticking the rag in his pocket. He opened a small fridge and pulled out a bottle of water, offering it first to Genny and then Josh. Both declined. The old-timer sat on a wooden bench that had seen better days. He took a deep pull from the bottle then turned to them.

"This about the other day?" At Genny's nod, he continued. "Been doing this job for twenty-five years. Not because I need to. Got a pension from the government that covers all my expenses. Nope, I took this job because driving the stagecoach is fun. No stress. Gets me out of the house and out from underfoot of the missus. Twenty-five years, and ain't nothing like this happened before."

Genny sat on the bench next to Hank. "We're hoping you might be able to help us."

"Don't know how. But I'll try."

"I read the statement you gave to Nick." Josh sat on a stepstool with his legs extended and feet crossed. If anyone saw them, it would look like three friends chatting. Nothing more. "Can you tell us what happened? Tell it like you told your wife or how you'd tell a friend."

"Sure," Hank said. "Well, it started out like any other trip. Got all the passengers and Genny loaded up inside. We took off, and I was enjoying the sun on my face and watching out for anything that would spook the horses. We were about two miles out, which is where the trail gets tricky. Lots of scrub, cacti, and boulders around. When I saw the horseman, I pulled up and stopped."

Hank took a moment to wet his whistle. While he did that, Josh took a moment to watch Genny, who was staring at something outside. He tried to see what but didn't notice anything unusual. Her brows pulled tight, creating vertical grooves in her forehead. Was she recalling her experience, or did something Hank say seem off to her? He'd ask later.

"Did you see the other two men right away?" Josh asked.

"Not until the first guy pointed them out. I wasn't gonna resist after that, because I was afraid they might have guns trained on us."

"Guns!" Genny sat up with her back pushed against the wall. "When he said the others would bring 'firepower,' I thought he was just playing around."

"Well, I wasn't so sure. And that's when the fella on the horse told me to stay put then proceeded to rob you all."

"Did anything about the guy on the horse seem familiar to you?" Josh remembered Genny saying she felt like she should know the man.

Hank slowly shook his head before lifting his gaze. "My attention was on those men in the trees, making sure they didn't get nervous. I sat there, staring at those trees, praying."

"You did the right thing, Hank. You kept your passengers safe. Nobody could ask more of you than that."

"Thank you, Josh. You always were a kind person. When that one fella was done, the other two met him at the edge of the trees and they rode off. That's when I saw the Prickly Pear brand on the other two horses. And then I relaxed and didn't think any more of it until we got back to the stables."

"Why did you relax?" Genny asked.

"That's when I figured the whole thing really must be an act. I'm not always told about changes in the scripts. I'm just a stagecoach driver."

"Hank, don't feel bad. I thought the same thing, and I'm often not told about changes either." Genny reached over and squeezed his arm.

"Thanks, Genny. That's nice of you to say."

"Did you notice anything else?" Genny asked.

"No, it didn't last long, although at the time, it felt like I was sitting there for an eternity."

Josh leaned forward. "What about in the days just before the holdup? Anything out of the ordinary happen? Did anyone ask more questions than usual?"

Hank scratched his neck as he squinted and focused on nothing in particular. Neither Josh nor Genny rushed the man. After a few moments, Hank's face lit up. "It's been business as usual with the passengers, with none of them acting suspicious and all, but a couple of days ago, something happened. We were on the morning run. You know, when it gets hot I only take the coach out twice a day so that the horses don't get sick."

Josh nodded and understood the heat that filled Hank's voice. There were some tour operators who ran the same set of horses from morning until night, with few breaks between tours, and treated the animals poorly. Hank babied his team.

"Anyway, I saw a couple of riders last week. Not that seeing riders is unusual, except that these two just sat there on their horses. I waved, and they rode off. Figured they were from another outfit that had ridden too far. Maybe when they saw me they realized they'd strayed onto Prickly Pear property."

"You've been a lot of help, Hank. Thank you." Josh stood and held out a hand to Genny to help her up. She took his hand, but they both knew she didn't really need the help. It was an excuse to hold her hand, if only for a few seconds.

Hank put his water bottle on top of the fridge then pulled the rag out of his pocket. "I need to get this old girl shined up for this morning's tour. I was real thankful the boss canceled yesterday's runs. I know we need to get back to business, but I have to admit, I'm a little leery myself."

"What if I rode with you?"

"That's mighty nice of you, Josh. I doubt many outlaws would hold up the coach with Doc Holliday on board."

Josh walked Genny to the café then slipped off to his one-room cabin. After they'd left Hank, Josh had asked Genny if she'd remembered anything new or if Hank's story seemed off. She'd said no, other than it had brought the incident back in living color. Once in his room, he powered up his computer and logged into the resort's system. His gut told him Hank was in the clear, but he needed solid proof. He hadn't seen hide nor hair of Hank on the guest room floors. Josh pulled up the reservation records for the stagecoach and riding lessons, which Hank gave in between tours. Then he pulled up the information Nick had given him on customer complaints about missing items, when the incidents occurred, and the probable locations based on the guests' recall of last seeing those items.

In each instance, Hank was busy at the stables, either with the coach or giving lessons. Just to be on the cautious side, he shot off an email to his coworker and asked her to run a financial report for Hank and Smitty. He had already confirmed Smitty's schedule the night before.

Once that task was done, he headed to the main building in search of the boss. Nick's office was behind the front desk, where he could quickly respond to guests' needs. Josh gave a quick knock on the door and walked in.

Nick looked up from his computer. "Josh, come on in and close the door. Please tell me you've figured out who's behind these thefts."

Josh did as he was asked. He wished he had better news to share. "Not yet. I've got my eye on a couple of people, but no proof yet." He crossed one ankle over the other knee, taking a moment to brush some dust off his boot. "This holdup has me concerned. It doesn't fit the previous pattern, and I don't know if it's the same culprits."

"You think I've got two different groups targeting me?" Nick leaned back, his hands pushing through his hair. "I can't take any more loss. I'm looking to bring in some investors. For almost fifty years, I've owned and run this hotel without outside help. It took every nickel I had, but I made it work. If word gets out, my investors will back out, and I'll have no choice but to sell or close."

"I understand what's at stake, and I'll do everything in my power to find who's behind all this. On that note, I have a few people that I know aren't involved, such as Genny Bowen."

Nick eyed him skeptically. "Do you have proof, or is that your heart talking? You two were quite the pair back in the day. It surprised me when she stayed after you left."

"Sir, I know Genny. She'd never do anything like this. If she was involved, that means she could never wear her necklace again, and it means too much to her and her mom. We ran a financial check on her before I even arrived. The only time there's been an increase in her deposits is when you've given her money for tuition. She's not involved."

"I agree. Like you, Genny means a lot to me. She's been a part of the PPR team for a long time. I wanted to make sure I wasn't looking through biased glasses."

Nick knew what the man meant. It was why he ran that report on Genny in the first place. This way, no one could accuse him of following his heart instead of his head, although both knew Genny wasn't involved. Still, he'd learned his first year as a PI, people only showed you the tip of their iceberg.

"With that in mind, I'd like to request permission to tell Genny the truth. Why I'm really here, what's happened, and how bad it truly is. She knows pretty much everyone working here. The staff loves her, and they're comfortable around her. And while you've given me access to the system, monitoring it takes time away from following up on other leads. If we loop Genny in, she can help in that area." It also gave him the perfect excuse for spending more time in her company, but Nick didn't need to know that.

The boss stared at him for a few moments, his finger tapping on the huge wooden desk separating the two. "Fine, but no one else. And Josh…"

"Yes, sir?"

"I need this wrapped up, and fast. Summer's almost over, and that's when the thefts stopped last year. The investors are coming in a couple of weeks, and I imagine if they're targeted, they won't want to invest in my hotel. Are you following me?"

"Yes, sir." Josh grabbed his cowboy hat and headed out to do more than play Deputy Doc Holliday. Three weeks ago, when Nick called the office of Arizona Security and Investigations, Josh's boss had hesitated to send him alone. At twenty-nine, Josh was a junior investigator compared to some of his coworkers, but he'd had a leg up on the others. He knew the Prickly Pear Resort from his years working there.

He had a plan. Help get the Phoenix office up and running with a solid track record. He figured a year, max. If his closed cases rate stayed on target, he'd be primed for a lead investigator role. LA, San Francisco, Seattle. He'd have his pick of offices to run. If he didn't solve this case, he could kiss his promotion goodbye.

∞ CHAPTER SIX ∞

The setting sun had left the Rusty Spur parking lot dark with the exceptions of those spaces closest to the building. There was just enough light that Genny could track Josh as he jogged back to the car where she waited. He had picked a parking spot that gave them an unobstructed view of the patio and, hopefully, of their mark. This was her first time visiting the restaurant, and if they hadn't been on a stakeout, she would have loved sitting out on the patio, with its soft lamps and strings of fairy lights overhead. They made for a perfect romantic setting.

He slid into the front seat of his Dodge Charger—not the best undercover car in Genny's opinion, but it fit with the other vehicles in the lot.

"Okay, we're all set inside," Josh said. "Now for the fun part... waiting."

When Josh asked if she minded an unconventional dinner, she didn't know he meant eating takeout while on a surveillance mission. Since he'd picked up tacos from her favorite restaurant, though, she didn't mind at all.

"They should be here soon. We better eat before then." She passed him a taco and then took a bite of her own, letting her eyes drift shut as an explosion of flavor took place in her mouth. The combination of fresh salsa, cool homemade crema, and spicy shrimp couldn't be beat. "I forgot to ask. How did the stagecoach run go today? You did both runs again, right?"

"Yep, and everything was how it should have been. Alice Wilkes regaled the passengers with stories from the Old West and pointed out the wildlife, and we returned to the resort both times without incident."

"Is it wrong that I'm disappointed?"

Josh shifted in his seat where he could see her and the restaurant. "Not in the least. I didn't expect anything would happen so soon after, but I hoped they'd try. Maybe my presence deterred them."

"Or maybe it was a one-time thing, and they've moved on."

"Don't worry, Genny. I'll find your necklace."

The reminder brought a fresh sting of tears to her eyes, but she refused to cry in front of Josh. For over a hundred years, mothers had entrusted and passed that necklace down to their daughters, sharing a bit of their family history, and Genny had lost it. She should have refused to part with it even for the short ride back to the resort. If they didn't find it soon, she was going to have to tell her mom. Not for the first time in the past few days, Genny said a prayer asking for help in solving the case and in returning everyone's property.

She finished her tacos and glanced at the clock on the car dash. Mac should arrive soon. "You were in there for a long time. What were you doing?"

"I paid the hostess to sit Mac and whoever he meets at a specific table outside, where I placed a recording device. We won't be able to hear the conversation until after they leave, but that's okay."

"You bugged their table?" Who was this guy sitting next to her? "Yep."

"How is it you know all this stuff? Bugging people? Stakeouts? Did you take an elective in law school or just watch too many cop shows?"

Josh chuckled. "Funny story. I did major in pre-law, with a minor in criminal justice, as planned. At the end of four years, I was sick of school. Going to law school meant going into debt for the next twenty years. Not something I wanted. Instead, I took what I'd learned and put it to work."

"Did you join the police force like your grandfather?" Genny could picture Josh in his dress blues and knew he'd cut a dashing figure.

"No. A private investigator."

What? Shock robbed her of her voice. She opened and closed her mouth several times before she could speak. "And now you're working at the Prickly Pear...just in time for a holdup. Something we've never had before. Josh, what's really going on?"

Before he could respond, headlights cut through the parking lot and across Josh's face. He picked up the binoculars.

"Bingo. There's Mac, right on time." Together, they watched him go inside. A few seconds later, another car pulled into the parking lot and a man climbed out. After what seemed like hours, Mac and the new guy followed the hostess outside to the table that Josh had bugged. "Perfect. The recorder is voice-activated, so we're good to go. After they leave, I'll go retrieve it." Josh picked up a camera with a long-range lens and shot a couple of pictures. He showed the digital photos to Genny. "Do you recognize the guy he's with?"

"No. Do you?"

"No, but that's fine. I can send it to a colleague to do a search. However, the recording might tell us more." He set the camera down and turned to her. "Where were we? Oh, yeah. What's really going on."

Josh filled her in on the thefts that had started toward the end of last summer then started up again this summer. As well as the fact that her boss had been paying off the guests out of his own pocket so that they wouldn't report the loss to the police and he didn't have to file a claim with the insurance company. Not exactly a win-win. Josh didn't know the full story, other than Nick was worried about some potential investors he wanted to bring in.

Genny took a few minutes to process the information. Tombstone, like most tourist destinations, had its problems with petty crime. But she'd honestly thought the Prickly Pear didn't have a security issue. Boy, had she been wrong.

"Are you mad I didn't tell you everything up front?" Josh asked.

Genny shook her head. "You were doing your job, keeping your promise to a client. Besides, I never asked about your job, just why you were in town. Saying it was a temporary thing and helping a friend wasn't a lie."

Josh leaned in closer, giving her a whiff of his aftershave. Apples, something citrus, and a spice she couldn't quite name. Whatever it was, the combination worked and made her want to move closer.

"Thank you for understanding." Josh brushed his pinky slowly, softly, over the back of her hand resting on the center console.

"Josh, you've always been one of the most honorable people I know."

Genny wanted to flip her hand over and lace their fingers together. She wanted to hold on tight. She wanted to never let go. Instead, she focused on the patio, on Mac, and on the surveillance, because she didn't know if what she felt was residual emotions. A sweet trip down memory lane. Or if this was the older, wiser, braver Genny falling all over again for the sweet neighborhood boy with the big plans.

While they waited for the meeting to end, they talked about old friends, family, and a little of Josh's life in New York before moving back to Arizona. New York sounded crazy busy yet fascinating at the same time. Maybe one day she'd take a weekend trip to the Big Apple. It would be fun to see Times Square, the Empire State Building, and the Statue of Liberty, but she didn't think she'd love the crowds or noise and people at three in the morning. She was quite the grump if she didn't get a full night's sleep.

Josh picked up his camera. "Here we go. They're leaving. I'm going to see if I can get a closer shot of Mac's friend. I'll give it a minute or two after they leave to retrieve the recorder."

Genny shifted in her seat, scooting closer to the windshield to get a better look. The two men came out, shook hands, and then walked to their respective cars. If it hadn't been for the holdup and Mac's strange comments on the phone, she wouldn't think their dinner was unusual at all. For all intents and purposes, they appeared to be two friends who met up for a meal and were now going their separate ways. Mac hadn't brought a bag or case full of stolen goods. They hadn't seen the mystery man slip him an envelope full of cash.

"I'll be right back. Keep the doors locked. Okay?"

She nodded and tried not to roll her eyes. Josh had a protective streak as wide as the Arizona sky. He crossed the parking lot, looking like any other patron on his way to dinner, but instead of going through the front door, he slipped between two planters lining the patio. He waved at someone—probably the hostess—then sat at the table Mac had occupied. A few seconds later, he exited the patio the same way and climbed into the car.

"Got it." He pulled his laptop from the back seat and downloaded the file. "Ready to hear what they were talking about?"

Genny stared at the recorder for a moment. What if Mac was involved? She wasn't his biggest fan, but she couldn't help feeling like she was intruding on his personal life. She laid her hand on top of Josh's arm. "Wait. If we find out he had nothing to do with the thefts, what are you going to do with the recording?"

"Delete it. Would you rather I listen to it alone and then let you know?"

Might be a good idea. Then again, with the way Mac had been acting lately, she really wanted to know what was going on with her boss. "No, I want to hear it."

Josh clicked the arrow.

"Thanks for meeting me out here," Mac said.

"No problem. We wouldn't want you to get fired before we're ready for you to leave."

"I'm ready to leave as soon as you say it's a go. I've done all I came here to do. I've got no ties to the area. What you're offering has so much more potential for bigger opportunities."

They listened in silence, but Genny's mind was abuzz. She couldn't believe what she was hearing.

"After our meeting the other day, I called my client. They were impressed with your skill set and ideas. They definitely want you on board. A formal offer should be in your inbox in the next week or so."

The two talked about details and timing before moving on to mundane topics. Genny only half listened as she processed the conversation. When the recording ended, Josh hit delete, as promised.

"Not what I was expecting," he said.

Genny shook her head as she stared at nothing in particular. Mac was planning to leave the Prickly Pear. He hadn't met someone to pawn stolen goods. He'd met a headhunter. She couldn't really picture Mac O'Neal, the man who had perfected his scowl, working for a theme park in Orlando. Not just because of his cloudy disposition. The man hated the heat. As soon as the temperature touched the eighty-degree mark, he started complaining. Basically, from April until November, her boss acted like the Wicked Witch of the West doused in water.

"We can now cross Smitty—who is legit sick, Hank—who's been nowhere near the hotel rooms and was out with gallbladder surgery last summer when things were going down, and now Mac off the suspect list."

"Who does that leave us?" Wow. Possibly no more Mac in her life. The thought made her almost giddy. She crossed her fingers and said a little prayer, asking for Mac to get the job. Not just because she'd benefit from it but because it had been clear on the recording that her boss was as miserable as he made the people around him.

"There's still Shane and Colby. Nick gave me access to the security cameras. I've seen the two of them all over the resort, but not once have I seen them on the guest floors. Maybe that housekeeper, Anna, is working with them."

"But none of them worked at the resort last year." She glanced Josh's way, only to see him frowning as he tapped his fingers on the steering wheel. "How does that work?"

"What if it's a ring?" His fingers stopped tapping. He turned to her. "What if the Prickly Pear isn't the only target? I've been thinking about this. It could be a group, and they rotate targets and players each year, so this year's crew is at a new place and therefore not suspected of the previous year's crimes."

"I think it's a little scary, and we probably need to get the local police involved. If it is a ring and they're hitting other resorts in Tombstone, those places might have reported the thefts. The police might have more information that could help."

"Yeah, except Nick has forbidden me to talk to the police. My hands are tied."

Josh drove out of the parking lot, headed to her apartment. His fingers tapped the steering wheel again. She left him to his thoughts. When he was ready, he'd share. In the meantime, she had her own to sort through. The last few days with Josh… It was like coming home after a long trip. She still wasn't sure what kind of future they could have or if this was a passing thing. She cared about him— deeply—and she imagined she always would. Josh made her laugh and feel safe and confident, and he respected what she had to say. If Nick offered her Mac's job, she'd be stuck in Tombstone, and Josh would be three hours away. That's if he offered her the job. He'd passed her over the last time. Did she even want Mac's job now?

CHAPTER SEVEN

Four days had passed since the Great Holdup. Not that anyone else called it the Great Holdup, but in Genny's mind, especially deep in the night, that's all she could call it. While she and Josh had ruled out a few suspects, they still didn't have any solid leads. They'd had one complaint the day before of a missing tablet. But it turned up at the pool with the guest's teenage daughter. Thankfully, or not, it had been quiet since Monday.

Good for business. Not so good for Genny's quest to find her missing necklace.

Another thing to be thankful for—truly thankful—they'd had fewer people call in sick and a fully booked resort for the weekend, both of which lifted a weight from her shoulders. Maybe she could finally catch up on paperwork. She'd just pulled up the time sheet reports when a knock at her door had her looking up.

Josh stood in the doorway, his shoulder pressed against the frame with a to-go cup in one hand and a white takeout bag in the other. "Hope I'm not interrupting."

Genny glanced at her screen then hit the sleep-mode button. "Not at all. What's up?"

He set the cup and bag in front of her. "I noticed that you usually stop by the café for a late breakfast, but you didn't this morning."

"I had a meeting with Nick and Mac."

He'd noticed her routine? And when she deviated? A small thrill ran through her. She peeked into the bag to find her favorite muffin—lemon poppy seed—and her heart melted. She popped the lid from the to-go cup and took a sip of sweet iced tea with lemon. Not only had he noticed her routine, but he'd remembered her favorite food and drink.

He closed the office door, giving them privacy. "A meeting? Anything I should know about?"

She took another sip. "No, except that Nick has some investors visiting soon and everything better be perfect or heads will roll."

Josh dropped into the leather chair across from her. His neck popped and cracked as he rolled it, then his shoulders. As frustrated as she was from the loss of her necklace, he had to be feeling even more so, since it was his actual job to catch the bad guys.

"In other words, we better solve our mystery."

"Yep." This close, it was easy to see the fine lines around his bloodshot eyes and stress lines along the sides of his mouth. As much as she was dying to eat her muffin, he looked like he could use it more. She pulled it out of the bag and held it up. "Want half?"

Josh shook his head. "I'm good. Thanks. You should eat though."

Genny took a bite because she was starving and he'd gone to the trouble of bringing her breakfast. "Oh, I almost forgot. Anna, the housekeeper, called in and said she would be out sick today."

"I know Marta is adamant that Anna is not involved, but I think we need to look a little deeper at her. My team in Phoenix is doing background checks on all the resort's employees. I'll ask them to move Anna's toward the top. Maybe you could mention her to your mom and see what she has to say about her former student."

"Um. My mom?" Suddenly, her whole body itched as her stomach cramped. She'd been avoiding her mom for days now. "Can we leave that as a last resort?"

"Why?" Josh asked, but a few seconds later his eyes opened wide as he reached back and massaged his neck muscles. "You haven't told her about the necklace yet, have you?"

"Nooooo." She dropped her head into her hands. "I was hoping I wouldn't have to tell her. If I go over there and I'm not wearing it, she'll ask why not."

"Could you call her?"

"Sure, but then she's going to ask why haven't I stopped by." She blew out a deep breath. "I have to tell her, eventually. Let me see what I can do."

Maybe she could do a quick video call? The lost necklace wasn't the only thing keeping Genny from stopping by to see her parents. For the past week she'd been pulling double shifts, helping out where they needed an extra body at the resort. Not only had she filled in on the stagecoach but also the front desk, the concierge, stocking shelves at Maisy's Mercantile, and busing tables at the Sarsaparilla Café. She'd helped set up movie night under the stars, and she'd run the kids' game night. Except for last night, she'd been going straight home and falling asleep as soon as her head hit the pillow.

"Are you sure? I don't want to put you in a tight spot with your mom," Josh said.

"It's okay. I still have to dig into Shane's and Colby's files. I took a quick look the other day. Nothing popped out except they didn't list any references. I asked Mac about it, but he told me the barn staff wasn't his problem."

"After his meeting last night, he's probably working with one foot already out the door."

"Pretty sure that's his standard MO." If the man had another way of operating, Genny had yet to see it, and she'd worked under Mac for the past two years.

"Any word on Smitty?"

"He's still in the hospital. Mrs. Smith hopes he'll get released tomorrow, but he won't be back to work for at least a week after he gets out."

She scribbled a quick note. *Smitty—Get-well basket.* If she waited a day or two after the hospital released him and hand-delivered the gift, it would be the perfect time to get some info on the two stable hands. Actually, knowing Smitty, he'd probably drill her on everything that had happened with him gone. It would be the perfect cover for snooping.

"I've been going through security footage at night. So far, I haven't found any evidence that they've been on the guest room floors. They've been everywhere else."

"What do you mean?" Genny's head snapped to attention.

"Just that they seem to always be coming or going somewhere. I've spotted them behind the café talking with the cooks a few times. And another time, I walked into the mercantile and Shane was chatting to the cashier, but as soon as he saw me, he shut up. Then Colby was over by one of the linen delivery trucks."

"Why would he be near a linen truck?"

"Good question. I asked him what was up, and he said he was stretching his legs."

"There's something about those two…" Genny let the sentence hang because she really didn't know how to finish it. She wasn't sure how to describe her impression. Shady? Sneaky? Slippery?

"Yeah. They're up to something, I just don't know what. Right now, they're my top suspects, but until I find proof, that's all they are." Josh closed his eyes as he rested his chin on his palm. For a moment, Genny thought he'd fallen asleep.

"Did I keep you out past your bedtime last night?" He'd dropped her off after they left the Rusty Spur. While Genny had been tempted to work some more, she could barely keep her eyes open and went straight to bed.

"No, that's all on me. Like I said, I was reviewing security footage." He sat up straight with a smile tugging at his lips. "Last night was fun. We should do it again."

"Go on another stakeout? Sure, but who are we watching this time?"

Josh chuckled. "I was talking about going out together. On a date but a proper one this time. I'm off tomorrow night. What do you say? Dinner in an actual restaurant?"

A little disappointment washed over her. The stakeout had been fun. Who knew? Maybe she'd switch career paths and become a private eye. But the best part of the evening had been spending time with Josh. Talking. Laughing. Just the two of them again, like old times.

"It just so happens, I'm free tomorrow night."

"Perfect—"

"Genny…" Mac burst into her office and came up short when he spotted Josh. "Am I interrupting?"

"No." She slid a peek at Josh, who sat with his back to Mac as if he wasn't there.

"Then, Doc, don't you have anything better to do than to flirt with the boss?"

Josh stood, slow and easy, reaching for his hat that he'd dropped onto the other chair. He put it on then touched the brim. "Ma'am. You have a nice day now, you hear."

He turned to leave, but Mac blocked the doorway. Josh said nothing. A few seconds later, Mac scuttled to the side to let him out, and Genny had to bite down on the inside of her lip to keep from laughing.

Josh walked outside into the bright morning sun with a smile as wide as the Grand Canyon. One would think he had nothing to smile about. After all, he'd been on the Prickly Pear case for three weeks, and he had nothing to show for it. Well, that wasn't entirely true. He'd cleared a few names from the suspect pool. But he'd taken the job for two reasons. One, it was a paying job, and he'd owed Nick for giving him a start as a teen. And two—and this reason was just as important, if not more—it gave him a chance to see Genny again. To get to know the person she'd become over the years. To see if there was still a connection, a spark between them. And, based on the rosy-cheeked smile she'd given him when he'd asked her out again… He'd say there was definitely something there.

A family of four pulled up in front of the hotel's main entrance. As they piled out of the car, a little boy around eight pointed to him. "Mom, look. It's the sheriff."

Josh walked over and held out a hand to the kid. "Howdy and welcome to the Prickly Pear Resort. I'm Deputy Holliday, but you all can call me Doc." The kid shook his hand, and Josh helped the father unload the car, passing the suitcases off to the bellhop. After that, he touched the brim of his hat. "You folks enjoy your stay."

Summer was winding down, and yet, according to the front desk clerk he'd talked to, the resort was booked out for the next two months. If he could solve this case, Nick stood a good chance to see a turnaround in finances. Then again, if he'd get out of his own way and report the thefts to his insurance carrier, he wouldn't be in this predicament in the first place. But it wasn't Josh's job to judge. On most days, he succeeded, but it was hard in his business. He waved to a few folks as he made his way from the main resort building and down the sidewalk to the alley that would lead him to the staff cabins.

Josh planned to use his free time today to check in with the Phoenix office and do some deeper financial dives. He had just entered the alleyway when raised voices had him slowing his steps. He couldn't make out the words, but the tone was crystal clear. As he emerged from the alley, he spotted Ed and Alice Wilkes just as the wife drilled her index finger into her husband's chest. Whoa. He'd never seen the lady be anything other than pleasant. She had a kind word and a smile for everyone she met. Normally, the two could be seen strolling along Main Street with her arm linked through his. The perfect picture of a happily married couple. Not so right then.

He was about to turn around when Ed looked up and caught Josh's eye. Alice glanced his way, said something under her breath to her husband, and then stalked off past Josh. Ed hung back. For a minute Josh debated whether he should say anything or just keep walking. He wasn't the type to stick his nose into other people's business…at least not uninvited. But as the Wilkes's cabin was next to his, he'd talked a little to them here and there.

"Everything okay, Ed?" Josh asked.

Ed shot him a look that had Josh stepping back. "Do yourself a favor. Don't get married." The anger laced through his voice had Josh holding up his hands and mumbling an apology as Ed stomped off after his wife. Weird. Then again, who knew what really happened behind closed doors? Relationships took work. A lot of work.

Look at him and Genny. If you'd asked him when he'd left for college if he thought they'd break up, he would have laughed…long and hard. He had no idea how she'd felt deep down inside. Whether she'd been scared or thought his dreams had been more important than she was. He'd been blinded by what he saw on the surface, what he wanted to see. Maybe Genny knew him better than he knew himself or her back then. He'd like to think he would have put her needs, wants, and fears first, but to be honest, he'd been a headstrong dreamer and probably would have done something stupid like put himself first.

Hopefully, he'd changed. Or had he? If Mac got the job in Orlando, there was a high probability that Nick would promote Genny to HR manager. A position she'd worked toward for years. Even knowing that, Josh still planned to pursue what was developing between them now. Even knowing he had no plans to move back to Tombstone. Other than Genny, there was nothing in his hometown for him. His family had all moved to the Phoenix area. His job was in Phoenix, and Tombstone didn't have the population to support him opening his own office. What were his options?

Give up Genny again?

Work full-time at the resort as a character actor, getting paid a fraction of what he made working for Arizona Security and Investigations?

Or try to convince her that he was worth taking a chance on and moving away from her family?

Just thinking of option one had him pressing the heel of his palm to his chest as pressure built and constricted his breathing. He hadn't realized just how much he'd missed her over the years. Sure, he thought about Genny on a regular basis. Songs would trigger memories. Or he'd try a new restaurant and instantly think how much she'd love the place and food. Or he'd be watching a movie and something a character said would remind him of their conversations. And of course, his mom and sister would bring her name up in almost every conversation, enough that he'd broken down and checked out her social media. Seeing her smiling face had more memories and emotions flooding through him. That's when he knew. Life had been sweeter when Genny was a part of it.

He had a second chance. Now not to blow it.

He'd just reached his cabin when his phone pinged with a text. Time to put his life aside and get the job done. He pulled up a message from Heather Thomas, who worked in the Phoenix office with her husband, Eric. Both had been doing background checks for him while working their own cases.

Shane Rogers and Colby Summerton. Zero criminal records. Graduated Santa Rita High, Tucson. No Marriage records. No bankruptcy. No liens. Previous employment – Circle T Ranch, Mammoth, AZ. Do you want us to dig deeper?

Yes. Need to know about financials.

While Heather worked on the stable hands, Josh dug into the mysterious housekeeper, Anna Jacobs.

⁓ CHAPTER EIGHT ⁓

When Josh picked her up for their dinner date, Genny had no idea where he planned to take her, but the last place she'd imagined was the Longhorn. It wasn't that she didn't love their food, but it was smack-dab in the middle of tourist central. It sat on Allen Street. The road in front was closed off to all but foot traffic and stage-coaches. Before it was the Longhorn, it was a bunch of other establishments, making it the oldest continually operated restaurant in town. Again, she didn't hate the place, but she had hoped for something a little quieter, a little more romantic. Something with dimmed lighting, cloth tablecloths, and candles.

As expected, a line of couples and families snaked out the door and down the wooden sidewalk, waiting for tables. Josh led her to the hostess stand. He gave his name, and as Genny turned to go wait outside with the others, the hostess told them to follow her.

Genny shot Josh a questioning look.

"It pays to be Doc." His lips quirked up on one side. "Don't worry, we're not cutting the line. I made reservations."

They took their seats at a table in the back corner with a RESERVED FOR DOC HOLLIDAY sign on it. The hostess plucked the sign up and handed them menus, although Genny doubted either of them needed one.

"You couldn't pick a cheesier restaurant?" Genny shot him a smile with a slight shake of her head. Not only was it a mecca for tourists but the site of their first date.

"Hey, no one does barbecue ribs like the Longhorn."

"True. Bet you didn't get food like this in New York." Genny gave a quick once-over of the menu to see if anything new had been added before setting it down.

"You'd be surprised." Josh didn't even glance at the menu. When the waitress arrived with their waters, they both put in orders for ribs, sweet potato fries, and green salads.

"Tell me about New York. Was it exciting?"

Josh grinned. "At first it was, then it became just another city. More people. More traffic. Lots of tourists. Times Square is crazy. The week from Christmas to New Year's Eve, there are so many people you can barely walk."

"Doesn't sound like fun." It sounded like Genny's nightmare come to life.

"Under all the noise and the bright lights are people like you and me. People going to work, raising kids, chasing dreams, and just living their lives." A hint of wistfulness tinged his voice.

"Do you miss it?"

"A little. Not as much as I missed my family or…"

"Or?"

"You."

She had to fight from grinning like a lovestruck teen as heat flared across her cheeks. "I'm sure they're all thrilled to have you home."

"They are. As much as I liked New York and my job, it can be a lonely place, especially when you're from a big family."

"I thought you couldn't wait to escape the chaos that's the Mendoza household?"

Josh chuckled. "Yeah. What's that saying? You don't know what you have until it's gone. The holidays were hard. Thank goodness for video chats."

She couldn't imagine holidays without her family. Going to church on Christmas then coming home where they'd be joined by aunts and uncles and cousins galore. Or Fourth of July barbecues. Or spending her birthday with the people who meant the most to her.

"I don't know how you lasted as long as you did."

"When Jason and Lynn had their first child—Layla, who's two— that's when I realized it was time to come home. My parents would have let me have my old room, but that felt like moving backwards. I couldn't come home without a job lined up." The waitress arrived with their food, and Josh waited until she'd finish setting everything down.

"Last fall, the company I work for, which is a subsidiary of a larger international firm, announced it was expanding and Phoenix was one of its target cities. I was thrilled when I was picked to be part of the founding team. Right now, it's a small office. There are three investigators and an admin person."

"Do you plan to stay there?" The Josh she'd known had always had big plans, pie-in-the-sky dreams, and him working for someone else seemed out of character.

"Someday I hope to either head up the office or start my own firm. For now, I'm the junior investigator, so I'm learning everything I can to be successful. Let's talk about you. Tell me everything you've been doing."

"Everything?" She glanced down at her plate then back up. "This is going to be a long dinner."

"Okay, fair enough. When we last left off, Genny Bowen had dreams of going to college, getting her degree in business management, and becoming a hotel manager. Is that still the goal?"

She took a bite of her salad as she thought how to sum up her life. The word *unfulfilled* came to mind, especially when she thought of all Josh had accomplished. But then she remembered something she'd heard in church. Everyone's journey was their own and shouldn't be compared to others.

"It's still the goal, although some of it is coming along slower than I had hoped."

"What are you talking about? You're twenty-seven and already in management. I think that's fantastic."

She ducked her head as the blush rose in her cheeks again. "Thanks. I just finished my associate's degree. I've had to go slow, taking one class a semester, because I'm also working full-time. I'd like to move up in management. I have so many ideas on how we can improve guest relations but, honestly, I think Nick looks at me and still sees that sixteen-year-old kid who just started at the hotel."

"He promoted you to assistant human resources manager. That means he has faith in you."

"Maybe, but instead of promoting me to HR manager, he hired Mac."

"Have you thought about going elsewhere? Someplace other than Tombstone? You know they don't hold the monopoly on hotels?"

She laughed and waved a sweet potato fry at him. "Are you sure about that?"

"Yeah, I'm pretty sure."

"Actually, I did consider applying to other hotels. But they all want someone with a four-year degree, even Nick. And I did think about moving, but Tombstone is home. My family has been here for almost a hundred and fifty years. I'm not as brave as you, Josh."

Josh reached over and squeezed her hand. "I have faith that whatever you put your mind to, you'll do it and be great."

She let Josh's confidence in her, along with his smile and the warmth from his hand, fill her from her toes to her nose. She'd missed this part of their friendship. Just being able to talk about anything and everything, about her hopes and dreams and her fears. She should have had more faith in him and their love all those years ago.

While she wanted to discover who was behind the thefts and get her family necklace back, she wasn't in a hurry to see this case come to an end. She wanted more time with Josh, time to let this renewed friendship flourish, and time to figure out if they even had a future together.

Slowly, she let go of Josh's hand and returned to her meal. As they ate, they continued to talk about friends they'd known, more about his life in New York, and some of the cases he'd worked as well as fun guest stories. They had just ordered an apple cobbler to share when Josh leaned in close.

"Don't look now—" He grabbed her hand to keep her attention. "I said don't look, but Shane and Colby just walked in with another guy."

Talk about a buzzkill. Up until the moment when he'd spotted the stable hands, Josh had forgotten the real reason he was back in Tombstone. They had slipped quietly into their old rhythm, supporting each other's goals and dreams, teasing, confiding, laughing, and basically just being Josh and Genny again. Not exes. Not coworkers. Not investigators. Friends.

A lightness he hadn't felt in years filled his soul.

It was like coming home.

Not because of the place but because of who he was with.

But with that one arrival, everything changed. His investigator's brain clicked back on. Who was the third member of their party? And wasn't that an interesting coincidence that their numbers matched that of the bandits? Except coincidences rarely happened. According to their personnel files, Shane and Colby were thirty-nine and thirty-five respectively. The new guy looked like another wrangler—mid-to-late thirties, medium height, fit, with short, curly black hair, and dressed in worn boots, jeans, and a blue plaid shirt.

Josh tracked their movement as the hostess led them to a table. He paid close attention to their body language and vibe. Colby and the new guy chatted, all smiles and head nods. Shane led the way, his gaze bouncing around the room until it landed on Josh and Genny. He held Josh's gaze then gave a slight nod of acknowledgement.

When the trio sat down, Shane took the seat facing them. A few seconds later, both Colby and the new guy looked their way. Colby waved then turned back to his friends.

To everyone else, it looked like nothing more than a couple of people who knew each other saying hi. To Josh, it was a chess move and a challenge. Who would capture the other's king first?

Genny leaned forward. "What do you think they're doing here?" She whispered even though there was no need, as the trio were across the room and the restaurant was at capacity.

"You mean besides eating?" He and Shane locked gazes. "Plotting to take over the world? Better question. Do you recognize their companion?"

Genny glanced over at the table for a moment. "No. He looks a little familiar, like I've seen him around town but not at the resort. Does it look like they're waiting for someone?"

"Not really, and if so, it would be only one, based on the table."

"It's funny that there were three bandits and there's three of them. But if we're going on the assumption that whoever targeted the resort last year is behind this year's thefts, I don't see how they could be responsible. None of them were at the Prickly Pear last year."

"They could have been targeting a different resort."

Genny put her elbow on the table and cradled her chin in her palm. "Then where are the others in this hypothetical ring, and who is the ringleader?"

"Now you're asking the right questions. The security footage I've reviewed for the guest room floors looks like business as usual. Housekeepers pushing carts, going in and out of rooms at the right times, bellhops carrying luggage to rooms, food service delivering meals. Nothing pops as being out of the ordinary, but guests have complained that valuables have gone missing from their rooms. Housekeeping was the first department we ran background checks on. No one surfaced as being suspect."

Genny's scowl as he talked didn't surprise him. She'd been at the Prickly Pear for a long time. As the assistant HR manager, it was her job to review applicants. So if the thefts were an inside job, she'd feel responsible for hiring bad seeds. And she'd always been fiercely loyal to her friends and those she cared about. He couldn't help but wonder if he still qualified as part of her inner circle and if she'd defend him if he was accused.

"Not surprised, with Marta as the manager. She's one tough cookie who doesn't miss a thing. I know she's not involved."

"My gut says the same, but to be sure, we did a full dive into her life. She's happily married, has two grown children and three grand-children. Husband is a physician's assistant at the hospital. He's been there thirty years. They paid off their house three years ago. They live within their means, with low credit card balances on two cards. They've paid one car off, and Marta drives a new car they purchased last year with a loan through the credit union. Solid, sta-ble, hardworking—"

"Honest people," she interrupted. "I've been to Marta and Carlos's house. They're good people."

"Agreed. So, moving on. One difficulty in pinpointing people of interest is that we have staff who work multiple jobs. For instance, Alice Wilkes is the stagecoach docent, but in between runs she works in the gift shop and has filled in for a few other roles. And she's not the only one."

The resort organizational chart had too many overlaps, which was great for Nick's bottom line but a pain for Josh to figure out who belonged where.

"Over the last few years, Nick's been running the resort on a lean staff. We can't afford for people to be sitting around. You're one of the few with free range."

Josh laughed. "Free range? Makes me sound like a chicken."

Genny smiled as she rolled her eyes. "You're anything but a chicken. It takes bravery to do what you do."

They'd been nibbling away at their apple cobbler as they talked, but now it was gone and the waitress was back with their check. Genny was almost tempted to order a second dessert to prolong the date and spy on Shane and Colby. While they waited for the waitress to return with Josh's credit card, she asked, "What's next?"

"Hopefully, we talk with Anna from housekeeping tomorrow."

"Doubt that's going to get us the answers we're looking for. I talked to my mom today, and she raves about Anna. She also said to tell you hello."

Thoughts of Mrs. Bowen filled Josh with warmth. She'd been like a second mom to him during his teen years. Before he headed back to Phoenix, he needed to make a point of stopping and seeing both Mr. and Mrs. Bowen regardless of what happened or didn't happen with Genny and him.

"Did you tell her about the necklace?"

"Not yet. I'm still hoping I won't have to until after it's been found," she said.

"We'll find it, and we'll talk to Anna. You never know, she might have seen something out of the ordinary. My team is still running background checks, going deeper on the staff. I'll keep going through security videos and monitoring the stables. And I want you to review personnel records, especially for those who started last year and have returned for this season or stayed on full-time."

"What exactly am I looking for?"

"Anyone who acts nervous or seems to partner up with another employee or shows up in locations they have no reason to be." Josh wanted Genny tucked safely away in her office where she would be far away from any potential danger.

As they walked to the door, he glanced one last time at the mysterious trio, who appeared focused on their conversation.

Genny leaned into Josh. "Too bad we don't have one of your handy-dandy little recorders right now."

Chapter Nine

Genny paced the hallway outside of the costume room, waiting for Josh to change into Doc Holliday's garb. She'd been waiting all morning for him to show up for work as she reviewed personnel records looking for persons of interest with no luck. A person could only learn so much from a file, but she didn't want to surveil anyone without Josh. He was the trained professional, and she had to admit, he made her feel safe when he was around.

The costume room door opened, and Genny pounced on Josh as soon as he stepped out. "Finally! Where have you been all morning?"

"Is everything okay?" Josh scanned her from head to toe with a worried look.

"Anna is working today, but she's already halfway through her shift. Come on, she's working on the fifth floor." Genny grabbed his hand and pulled him to the service elevator. She jabbed the up button. She didn't want to let go of Josh, which was precisely why she did. Last night, when he'd dropped her off at home, he didn't kiss her good night, not even a peck on the cheek. He simply squeezed her hand and walked away. She was more confused about them than she'd ever been. "So why the late start today?"

"After I left you, I drove back to town, looking for Shane and Colby. They had just left the restaurant. I wanted to see where they'd go."

"And?" The word came out sharper than she intended, but she'd tossed and turned a lot last night.

"The three of them went into Big Nose Kate's Saloon. Stayed for about two hours. I was ready to give up when they finally left. Thankfully, it's tourist season, so I could follow them without their noticing. They walked to a small house a few blocks away on North 5th Street. I checked the records, and it's a rental property."

"Do you still think they're our bandits?"

"They're at the top of my list. I went back this morning and watched the house. Colby and Shane left first. I presume they came into work, because their Jeep is in the employee lot. The third guy came out about an hour later. I followed him. Looks like he might work for one of the tour companies in town. After that, I had a meeting with my boss. He's pushing to close this case, as he has others lined up and needs me in Phoenix ASAP."

He's leaving. The words played over and over in her head. *It's too soon. He can't leave. We haven't solved the case. He promised he'd get my necklace back.* As if that was really what mattered the most. For over a decade she'd lived without Josh in her life, never fully realizing what she'd given up until he'd returned, and now he planned to leave again. Pressure built behind her eyes, tingling, but she refused to become a sobbing mess in front of Josh or anyone else. She squeezed her eyes shut, willing the sensation to pass. The elevator door opened. Josh touched her arm, and her eyes flew open.

"Everything okay?" he asked.

"Yep." She stepped forward, coming even with the man who was going to break her heart. "Sounds like we better get busy and solve this mystery." She ignored Josh's piercing eyes and the way he tilted his head, watching.

She strode down the hallway until she came upon the housekeeper's cart. She peeked inside the nearby room, spotting their target. She knocked on the open door to get the girl's attention.

"Hi, Anna?" Anna looked up from making the bed, startled. "I'm Genevieve Bowen, from human resources, and this is Joshua Mendoza. We'd like to ask you a few questions."

"Sure, Ms. Bowen. What can I do for you?" Anna's gaze bounced from her to Josh. She stayed perfectly still except for twisting her apron in her hands.

Josh leaned against the dresser, his arms crossed. If he was trying to set the girl at ease, she didn't think his pose would work. It reminded Genny of the one time her dad caught her skipping school.

"Did you enjoy your days off?" Josh's question sounded like an ordinary thing to ask a coworker, yet odd given the circumstances.

Anna looked up. "I guess, except I wasn't feeling well yesterday. I think I got that stomach virus that's been going around." She turned her attention to Genny. "I'm sorry I missed my shift."

"It's all right. This virus has hit every department. We're glad you're feeling better, but we wanted to talk to you about something else."

"Okay." Her voice was small and quiet.

"Wednesday, you were seen carrying a garment bag from the hotel to your car. Can you tell us what was inside?" Josh asked.

She twisted the apron around and around her hand. "I know I shouldn't have done it without permission, but I promise we were really careful—"

"Careful with what, Anna?" he asked.

"I borrowed a couple of dresses from the resort. My best friend and I were invited to this party, but you had to come in costume. I tried to find something, but everything was too expensive. But I promise, we made sure nothing got spilled on them, and we even had her mom clean them for us. I'm supposed to pick them up tonight."

Once she started talking, the whole story spilled out. Anna and her friend had pledged a sorority, and the party was part of the initiation. If they didn't show up in costume, they wouldn't be allowed in. Maybe Genny was glad she'd missed that part of college life.

"Please don't fire me. I really need this job to help pay for books and stuff. I'll do anything."

Taking costumes off property was against the rules, but Anna had a clean record with no reprimands or other offenses. As long as she returned the dresses clean and undamaged, Genny didn't feel it was a fireable offense. She'd still have to talk to Marta and let her know what Anna had done.

"Report to my office tomorrow before your shift starts. As long as you do your job and don't do anything to get in trouble for the next three months, this won't go into your personnel file."

Anna released the twisted cloth, her gaze finally meeting Genny's. "Thank you. I'll be there at seven sharp, and I promise, I'll be the perfect employee."

Genny turned to leave so Anna could get back to work, but Josh stayed put.

"Josh?"

"Hang on a minute." He held up a finger. "Anna, maybe you can help us out."

"Sure. Whatever you need." The girl's face brightened with hope.

"You started at the beginning of the summer, right?"

"Yes, I work here during the mornings and at the Tombstone Trading Company in the afternoon and evenings. I'm trying to save up enough so that I only have to work the weekends once school starts."

"Have you noticed anyone lurking around the guest rooms?"

"No. I mean, right now it's pretty quiet, but normally, people are coming and going all day long. Mostly I ignore everyone unless it's a guest needing to get back in their room while I'm cleaning or if one is asking for more towels or something."

"That's fine. Can I ask another question?"

Anna nodded.

"When you're cleaning a room, is it standard procedure to keep the door open?"

"Yes. We have to keep it open. That's Ms. Marta's rules. She said it's so no one can accuse us of doing anything wrong while we're in the room."

"Does everyone in housekeeping follow Marta's rules?"

The girl's eyes grew large. "If they want to keep their jobs, they do."

"Okay, that's helpful, thank you. Can you do us a favor? Can you keep your eyes open for anyone not following that rule? Or if you see anyone who doesn't look like they belong or seems suspicious, let me or Ms. Bowen know right away."

Anna agreed then returned to work as Genny and Josh walked down the hall toward the elevator.

"Do you believe her?" Genny asked.

"Yeah. You?"

"Either she was telling the truth or she's a talented actress and has missed her calling."

"I'll let you get back to work. Main Street and my fans are calling my name."

Genny bit her lip to keep from laughing. "Well, we wouldn't want to disappoint your fans, that's for sure."

Josh grinned at her. "Never. Oh, hey. Do you have a picture of your necklace?"

"There's a picture of me wearing it in the staff break room. Why?"

Josh hit the button for the first floor. "I'm going to check with a few pawnshops in the area and see if anyone has tried to sell it."

"I thought Nick said to keep this quiet."

The elevator doors opened, and they walked to the center of the lobby. Josh tucked a strand of loose hair behind her ear, letting his fingers caress her cheek as his hand dropped.

"I promised you I'd find your necklace."

Genny grabbed his arm. "Josh, don't do anything to jeopardize your job. You know Nick doesn't like to be ignored. If he finds out you went against his wishes, he'll fire you. It's not worth it."

"Genny, you are totally worth it."

He left Genny standing in the middle of the lobby and headed to the break room, where he snapped a photo of her necklace, zooming in close to get the details. He didn't want to argue with her. Josh meant what he said.

Last time, she put him and his dream first. She needed to know he would risk his job for her.

Time was running out. With only a couple of weeks left of summer, either he cracked this case now or not only would he let Genny down but Nick and his boss too. Watching employees had gotten him zero so far. It was time to expand his search. Nick may have not wanted to advertise the Prickly Pear's woes, but Josh needed to discover if the bandits had tried to unload their loot.

He took a stroll down Main Street, making a point of flirting with all the women and talking with the kids. He stopped in the Sarsaparilla Café for a quick bite then went through the kitchen to take a shortcut to his vehicle. As he came out the back door, he spotted Shane Rodgers talking to one of the vendors for Maisey's Mercantile. The guy passed something to Shane that he pocketed right when Josh made eye contact with him. Shane smirked and walked away. The vendor climbed into his truck and drove off before Josh could question him.

Josh couldn't question the staff at Maisey's without raising red flags. Every which way he turned, his hands were tied. Maybe it was time to bring in backup. He'd have to see if Eric and Heather could spare a couple of days. For now, he went back to the costume room, changed back into his own clothes, and headed into town and the nearest pawnshop.

A few hours later, he'd hit the shops in Tombstone as well as the stops along the way to Sierra Vista and down to Bisbee. His head pounded, his stomach grumbled, and he was no closer to solving the mystery than he'd been that morning. It was always possible the thieves took a trip to Tucson to unload their haul. It was an easy drive that took less than two hours.

He made a quick stop at a roadside food truck to grab a couple of carne asada burritos for dinner and headed to his cabin. He needed to check in with the office. What he really wanted to do was see Genny. See her smile. Hear her voice. Listen to her laugh.

She had a way of making the weight he carried on his shoulders feel lighter, more manageable, like he was Hercules. But he wanted to lift the burdens she carried. He knew that deep down she blamed herself for the thefts, that she felt it was her fault for letting unsavory individuals invade the Prickly Pear family and betray their trust. But what she considered a fault, Josh considered one of her greatest assets, and that was her ability to look for, and find, the good in people. It was why she gave Anna the housekeeper a second chance.

As Josh sat at the little table in his cabin, he bowed his head to say thanks for his meal and to ask God to help him find a viable lead.

CHAPTER TEN

It had been a quiet couple of days. There hadn't been a single complaint of missing property from any of the guests. Shane and Colby had been sticking close to the barn. The hospital released Smitty, but he was on convalescence leave until his strength returned. Anna hadn't made one step over the line nor had she seen anything odd.

Genny had shoved her worries aside and decided she and Josh needed a break. He'd picked her up at seven to beat the heat, and they headed to the San Pedro River Trail. By mutual agreement, they didn't talk about the case or their past.

They were at the point on the return trip that brought them along the river. It was one of the few places that offered shade, and she was ready for it. She slipped her hiking boots off and walked into the cool water. Because of a heavy rainy season, the water ran higher than normal and felt like paradise against the heat of the day.

"Come on, city boy. Or are you afraid of a little water now?" Genny removed the cooling cloth draped over her neck and dunked it into the water. She squeezed the excess before replacing it then splashing her face, instantly cooling off.

"Hardly." Josh dropped his backpack on the bank.

Genny scooped up a handful of water and tossed it at Josh, splashing his shirt. A silly, girlish giggle erupted, and she slapped a hand over her mouth.

"You're asking for it."

"Just having some good old-fashioned fun. You remember what that is, right?" She rested her hand on her hip and beckoned him to join her with the other.

Josh unlaced and kicked off his old hiking boots. They had seen better days and not a lot of use over the past few years. "It's been a while, but I think I remember."

He waded into the river until it reached his knees then leaned over and dragged his hand through the water. As he lifted his arm, he captured a handful of water that made its way through the air to spray Genny in the face.

She laughed. "Nice aim."

For the next several minutes, they splashed and played until they were both soaked from head to toe and laughing until neither could talk and Genny's stomach hurt. She held up her hands to form a *T*.

"Time out," she gasped, trying to catch her breath.

Josh got one last splash in. She eyed him and stepped forward with every intention of getting her revenge.

"Ow." She hopped on one foot. "I think I stepped on a sharp rock or something." She tried to put her weight on her right foot, only to jerk it up and almost fall.

Before she could take another step, Josh was there, lifting her. He carried her out of the water, up the short bank, and over to a picnic table set under a group of trees. He dropped to his knees in front of her and lifted her injured foot for inspection.

"Stay here." He ran to the riverbank and grabbed their backpacks and boots. "You've got a cut. Let me get it cleaned." He pulled a first-aid kit out of the pack, and with whisper-soft strokes, he cleaned the cut and then applied antibiotic cream and a bandage. "There you go. Good news. I think you'll live, but remember I'm not a real doctor, I only play an old-time dentist-turned-marshal."

She laughed as she inspected his handiwork. "Think it'll get me out of working tonight's reunion at the resort?"

Genny patted the spot next to her, inviting Josh to sit down. Their shifts didn't start for several more hours, and she wasn't in a hurry to end their morning together. The day had filled her heart and soul with light and joy. Out here, they were just Genny and Josh. Two locals enjoying the natural beauty that surrounded them. Outsiders might see a dusty trail surrounded by tall, dry grass and keep their gazes glued to the ground, looking for dangers of the desert, but she saw home. Freedom. Serenity. She saw God's masterpiece.

And there was no one she'd rather share that experience with than Joshua Mendoza, the man who had stolen her heart, not once but twice. She was pretty sure that even though she'd tried to keep her distance at first and build walls around her heart, she'd fallen for him all over again.

Years ago, as a silly boy of fifteen, he'd caught her attention with his mad soccer skills. She couldn't kick a ball straight to save her life, much less bounce one on her knee. He'd then stolen her heart when he saved her from having to dissect a frog, offering to do it for her and let her be the one to record the data. He'd been sweet, considerate, and gallant, always standing up for the underdog. Fast forward more than a dozen years, and she still found him all of those things and more.

"Penny for your thoughts."

Heat stole over her cheeks, and she hoped he believed it was just from the heat of the day and not because he'd caught her daydreaming about him. "They might be worth more than a penny."

"Will you take an IOU?" His smile reached his eyes. He bumped her shoulder with his. "You looked about a million miles away. Everything okay?"

Grown-up Josh was smart, charming, and irresistible, especially when he smiled like that at her. "Everything is perfect. Being out here, surrounded by nature and blue skies, and being with you. It'll be the best part of my day."

"I know what you mean." He rested his hand on the bench, his pinkie linked with hers. "I've missed this."

"What? They don't have hiking trails in New York?"

"Not like this. Plenty of concrete ones though." He leaned in close. "I'll tell you a secret, but you've got to keep it to yourself. They actually have lots of parks and trees in New York. There's even a river."

"Would you go wading in the Hudson?"

"You couldn't pay me to go in *that* river."

She chuckled. "Me either."

"I'm glad I came home to Arizona."

"Me too."

"I don't know how many varieties of birds we saw today."

"A lot. More than you'd see in New York, I bet."

"Yeah, and I spotted no less than four roadrunners today." His brows shot up as if seeing a roadrunner was the ultimate prize.

"Roadrunners are pretty cool. I can't imagine anything else topping your list." She held her breath as she searched his eyes for the answer she wanted to hear more than anything.

He slid his hand along her cheek, cupping her face. "I can. You, Genny, are at the top of that list." He leaned closer. Her mouth went desert dry as her pulse raced like a thoroughbred at Belmont. Then he kissed her softly.

Long-forgotten feelings zipped through her. Excitement. The promise of love. The giddiness of pure happiness. The joy of knowing she mattered to him.

He pulled back, but just far enough to give them breathing room as he rested his forehead against hers. "Do you think they'd notice if we didn't show up for work tonight?"

"Sadly, yes."

Josh sat up and laced his fingers with hers. "Genny, I need you to know that I never stopped caring about you. There wasn't a day that went by that I didn't think of you. I know I needed to get out of Tombstone, to see what the world offered, to find out what I was meant to become. My dream was to see more of the country, and I did, but my heart…it's always been in Arizona."

Genny's eyes welled up, but before he could do anything, she glanced at her watch. *Oh, man. What did I do?*

"We should get going. I promised my mom I'd stop by and see her before I go to work." She reached for her boots and pulled her socks out.

"Genny, wait a minute. I didn't mean to upset you. That wasn't my intention."

"I know. It's just that I feel guilty. I'm the one who broke up with you. I'm the one who didn't go through with our plans, not you. For years I've wondered if I made the right decision or not. And here you are being…being you. Understanding, honest, wonderful you. Not holding the breakup against me." She pulled her socks on with a bit more force than needed.

"Are you mad that I'm not holding it against you?"

She reached for her boots, slipped her feet in, and stomped on the ground. It made him want to retreat a step.

"How can I be mad at you when you're being so forgiving? I'm mad at myself. And I'm confused." She slipped her backpack on then headed down the trail.

Josh haphazardly tied his laces, grabbed his own backpack, and hustled after her. "Genny, talk to me. What are you confused about?"

She swung around to face him. Her cheeks glistened in the sun. "What am I supposed to do with that confession?"

"You don't have to do anything with it. It wasn't to make you feel guilty." He reached for her, and she stepped into his embrace, resting her head on his shoulder. It felt so right having her there, but he hated that he'd made her cry.

"I'm sorry," she said. "There's a lot going on in my head, and I'm just trying to make sense of it all. You did nothing wrong. Maybe my emotions are in a jumble because I'm going to see my mom today and I'll have to tell her about the necklace."

"I'll go with you. Be your wingman?"

She laughed as she wiped her cheeks on his T-shirt then stepped out of his arms. She slid her hand into his and tugged him forward on the trail. "Appreciate the offer, but I'm guessing you have video to watch and stable hands to spy on and other PI stuff to do. I'll be fine. I just need to figure some things out in my head."

"Okay, but if you want to talk, I'm here for you."

"I know." She stepped in closer, encircling his upper arm with her free hand.

They walked the rest of the way to the car like that, laughing, talking, connected. Now that he had Genny back in his life, he needed to figure out how to keep her there. If that meant giving her some time and space to think, he'd do it. But one thing he knew for sure. He wasn't letting her go without a fight this time.

CHAPTER ELEVEN

The Tombstone High reunion was in full swing. People packed the makeshift dance floor. Others kicked back at tables, catching up with old friends, and a few stragglers made another trip past the dessert table. Genny gave the band a ten-minute break. During which, the reunion committee would share updates on who had accomplished what over the past thirty-five years and then crown their king and queen for the weekend.

Genny slipped into a connecting room that they used for the staff. She wanted to make sure their snack and drink tables were full. She didn't need employees passing out. She snagged a bottle of water and had just cracked the cap when the outside door opened. Liz walked in, pushing a cart.

"Hey, how's everything going?"

"Good. People look like they're enjoying the party." Genny took a long drink. "The food looks amazing."

"Have you eaten anything?" When Genny shook her head, Liz handed her a half sandwich. Turkey and Swiss on sourdough. One of her favorites.

She dropped into an empty chair, happy to be off her feet for a few minutes. The cut on her foot wasn't giving her too much trouble. Still, what had she been thinking? Going on a ten-mile hike when she had a long night on her feet ahead. "Thanks. What about you?"

"Food? Who has time to eat? I've got people to feed."

Genny looked around the empty breakroom. "Looks like you've fed them. Grab something and join me. We haven't talked in days."

Liz selected her own sandwich and plopped into a chair. A groan escaped after she bit into her food. "I think this is the first thing I've had since six this morning. Thanks for reminding me to take care of me." She grabbed a bottle of water off the cart and pointed it at her. "Where were you this morning?"

Genny set her half-eaten sandwich on the table. The morning played back in her head, as it had done several times throughout the day.

"Stop biting your lip and talk," Liz said.

"Josh and I hiked the San Pedro River Trail, and then I stopped and visited with Mom."

Liz's eyes snapped open wide. "I'm not sure which one to ask about first. Let's start with your mom. There's probably less to unpack there."

"You're right. Mom's good. She's prepping for school to start while she enjoys the last few weeks off. She and Dad have taken up ballroom dance lessons."

"Really? What brought that on?"

"She said they were looking for something fun to do together. You know her. She can't sit still for long."

"Did you tell her about the necklace?" Liz whispered, even though they were alone.

A heavy wave washed through Genny. She had accepted that she might never recover her necklace, and she had to live with the idea.

Not that she had given up on Josh solving the mystery. She just didn't think the bandits would have held on to it for this long.

"I did, and you and Josh were right. She's just happy no one got hurt. Which reminds me. Have you heard any other tidbits from customers about missing property?"

"No, I haven't. I mean, nothing out of the ordinary. Guests are always leaving stuff behind."

Genny had left instructions with the front desk, the concierge, and housekeeping to alert her to any complaints. She'd have to check in with them, in case they forgot. She'd also check with the pool staff.

Liz reached over to the tray, snagged two brownies, and handed one to Genny. "Okay, so things are good at home. I'm going to guess that perplexed look had something to do with Josh. What happened on the hike?"

Sometimes having a best friend who knew you as well as you knew yourself wasn't a blessing. Genny filled Liz in on the hike and the conversation.

"Okay, I know you won't pull any punches. Am I being silly still hauling this guilt around after all this time?"

"Honestly?" Liz nodded. "Yeah, you are being silly. Hear me out. I've watched you and Josh do this complicated two-step for a good month now. You both obviously still have feelings for each other. And now he's told you he does. Other than missing you, does it seem like he's been suffering as he pined away for you all these years?"

"No." That was an easy answer. Josh loved his job, and he appeared happy about his life and how things turned out. Yes, he'd said that he'd thought of her every day, but he didn't say he sat in his apartment with a broken heart. They'd both moved forward, both reaching for their career goals.

"Okay then. Let the guilt go. I think you both needed the time away to find out who you are as individuals. Everything happens for a reason, you know. Now you know what you're capable of on your own and what you can really bring to a relationship. If you guys decide to give it another go, I think you'll totally rock it. Also, I'd like to remind you that I'm going to be your maid of honor and I despise the color orange. Unless it's a fruit."

Genny burst out laughing. "Good to know, but I think you're jumping ahead. Way ahead."

"Just putting it out there. Now, I need to go check the banquet table and see how the party revelers are doing. Wouldn't want them to run out of punch or cake." Liz gave her a quick hug and left. Genny cleaned up her mess as she let Liz's words marinate. Maybe it was time to let the past go and move forward. If Josh could absolve her of her past transgressions, so should she.

Genny said a quick prayer, thanking God for sending Liz to be her best friend and asking for strength and courage to follow her heart and not just her head.

Out in the ballroom, the former classmates clapped and cheered as a couple were crowned. From across the room, at the end of the dessert table, Liz gave her a thumbs-up to indicate all was well in her area. Several staff members quietly cleaned up discarded dishes, and the band retook the stage when the king and queen descended to the dance floor. Near the stage, Josh stood watching the crowd. He was in his Doc Holliday uniform, standing with a couple as they took a picture. His eye caught hers, and he nodded toward the doors.

"I must say, Miz Genny, you're looking mighty pretty tonight," he said once she joined him in the front hall.

She laughed and shook her head. "You're laying it on awfully thick, especially as no one else can hear you, *Doc.*"

"I don't care if they can hear me or not. It's the truth."

She'd stopped next to a welcome table that held four yearbooks spanning the graduating class's time at Tombstone High. She flipped one open, hoping Josh hadn't noticed the flush of her cheeks.

"Did you learn anything new today?" she asked.

"Not really. My team is almost done with the background checks. Not surprisingly, almost all of the younger employees have several social media accounts and share everything. Some of the older members have accounts, but they're more circumspect about what they share. Sadly, no one has posted any pictures of them in a bandit costume."

"Didn't think they would."

"Hey, it happens all the time." Josh put his finger on a photo, stopping her from turning the page. "Check out those fashions. Those are some bright colors."

"And big hair. This is why I tried to avoid the photographer in school. I didn't want to look back and wonder what had I been thinking."

Josh traced the curve of her cheek with one finger. "Do you have many regrets?"

His touch made her feel precious, loved, valued. She smiled, meeting his gaze. "I did, but I'm letting them go. A friend reminded me that things happen for a reason. I might have missed out on some stuff, but I don't hate my life or what I've done with it. I'm kind of proud of the person I am and..."

A slow, cautious smile lifted the corners of Josh's lips. "And?"

"I don't have all the answers, but I'm looking forward to seeing what comes next."

"Remind me to thank that friend sometime."

Genny barely registered Josh's comment. *This picture. The name. Coincidence? But it doesn't make sense.* Genny racked her brain as she tried to recall a detail that danced along the edges of her memory.

"Hey, what's wrong?" Josh asked.

"Look at this picture. Does she look familiar?"

"Alice Oswald? Never heard of her."

"Ignore the last name. Look at the picture instead." Josh focused on the yearbook photo, and his smile disappeared. "She looks like Alice Wilkes," Genny said. "That's weird."

"She does. Why is that weird?"

"Have you run their background checks yet?" Genny picked up the book for a closer look.

"She and Ed are in the next batch. Since they weren't new hires, they weren't priority."

"You might want to push them to the top of your list. At first, I couldn't remember why this picture bothered me. I mean, I know half the people in that room. But remember when Ed told us that he and Alice grew up and were married in Pittsburgh? If that's true, what is she doing in this yearbook?"

"Let's look for Ed," Josh said.

Genny flipped the pages until she came to the *W*'s, and yep, third row down, fourth picture over, was Edward C. Wilkes. The only thing the boy had in common with the man, though, besides a name, was he sported dark hair. "It doesn't look like him. Think the name is a coincidence?"

Josh took out his phone and captured a photo of both yearbook pictures. "More like thirty-plus years of living." He looked around, his gaze scanning the crowd in the other room. "Are they working the party?"

"No, they had today off. Personal reasons."

"Like avoiding old schoolmates who might spill their secrets."

His blood raced through his veins. It was this thrill, the pulse-pounding, heart-racing excitement that had hooked him on private investigating. Knowing he was close to unraveling a mystery sent a rush of endorphins pumping through his body. It was the same rush that adrenaline junkies felt when they pulled dangerous stunts, except Josh had better odds of succeeding.

He set the yearbook on the table and leaned in close to Genny. If anyone saw them, it would look like a private moment. "I'm going to head to my cabin. See if I can pull the research on these two and play connect the dots."

"What do you want me to do?" Genny's gaze darted all around. She had a terrible poker face.

"Do your job. If anyone asks for me, tell them I had to run an errand. If you run into Ed or Alice, act normal. Do not confront them. We don't have any proof yet, and we need more than a couple of pictures from the past."

She grabbed his hand as he turned to leave. "Josh, be careful. I know this is your thing, but don't let that tin star on your chest make you think you're invincible."

He cupped her cheeks and kissed her gently. "I'll be safe. Save the last dance for me."

Outside, the night temps had dropped to the mid-sixties and a cool breeze washed over him. After being in the overheated ballroom, it was a welcome change. He surveyed the resort. Families packed the arcade. More waited outside of the Sarsaparilla Café, waiting for a free table. Miss Maisey's Mercantile had a good number of guests shopping for last-minute souvenirs, snacks, and sundries. Everything was as it should be, except it wasn't.

Why was the barn light on? They'd brought the horses in hours ago for their final feeding and bedding down for the night. Nick didn't like them out at night where coyotes could get to them. The stable hands didn't work after the animals were in. Around eleven, a security guard made a last check, but it was only nine. Josh made a detour.

If anything funky was going on, he'd call for backup.

Josh did a perimeter check first. Not seeing anything out of the ordinary, he snuck around to the lit office window. Shane's and Colby's voices carried through the night, but not to where Josh could make out the conversation. He edged closer. Shane sat at the desk in front of the computer. Colby stood behind him. There was nothing odd about the stable hands being in the office. During Josh's second year at the resort, he'd worked in the stables. He frequently left Smitty notes on the horses' feed levels and such. Back then, Smitty didn't let other people touch the computer. Then again, he'd been out sick for over a week now. Maybe Shane and Colby volunteered to take on some of his work? Possible. Except why hadn't the task fallen to one of the other hands who'd worked there longer?

All good questions, but since whatever they were doing didn't appear to have anything to do with his case, he headed to his cabin. But he still couldn't shake the feeling that the two were up to no good.

Josh noted as he passed the Wilkes's cabin that all the lights were off. Where was the happy couple? He didn't have enough evidence to search their cabin, and without it, Nick would never give him the okay. Inside his own cabin, he dropped onto the wooden chair in front of his desk and pulled up the reports the Phoenix team had sent over earlier.

Ed Wilkes, age 53. Alice Wilkes, age 52. Married thirty-two years. No children. Last address listed as a rental in Pittsburgh. No police records, no liens, no lawsuits. He wrote down their birth dates and then skipped to the financial section. Decent credit score. A few credit card balances. Modest savings and checking account balances.

Nothing of interest popped out.

Josh kept digging.

He popped over to the personal details. Married thirty-two years, but where? His team hadn't included that info. He brought up another program and typed in their names and the year that they would have gotten married and paired it up with locations of Pennsylvania and Arizona.

And there it was.

One Edward C. Wilkes of Tombstone, Arizona, married Alice Oswald, also of Tombstone. Birthplace for both listed as Tombstone.

Why had they lied about their hometown?

And why were they missing their class reunion?

He needed more information.

Josh set up three more searches, this time through a private server. He hadn't run them before because of costs, but hopefully by the time the report finished he'd know what he needed to know about Ed Wilkes, Shane Rodgers, and Colby Summerton.

He'd done everything he could for the moment. On the way back to the main building, he noted the lights were still off in the Wilkes's cabin and so was the one in the barn office. The party was nearing the end, but the guests were still going strong. He spotted Genny leaning on a high-top table as the band announced the last dance.

He tapped her on the shoulder. "If you would be so kind, Miz Genny, I'd be honored to have this dance."

CHAPTER TWELVE

Saturday morning arrived way too early. All Genny wanted to do was snuggle into her pillow and fall back into her dream. She and Josh danced on the bank of the San Pedro River under a moonlit sky. Soft music played in the background, but from where, she had no clue. It was a dream, after all. It didn't take a psychology degree to figure out the why of the dream. Against her better judgment and best efforts, she'd fallen for Joshua Mendoza... again. It would be a wonderful thing if they didn't live three hours apart.

A half hour later she walked into Nick's office. It was his phone call with a demand for her presence that had awakened her from the dream. *So much for having the day off and getting to sleep in.* After a late night at work, Genny was just shy of irritable. Josh was also in the office. She dropped into the empty chair and mumbled hello.

"Thank you for coming in on your day off. Once we resolve this issue plaguing the resort, you've earned an extra-long weekend off with pay."

Genny raised her eyebrows and glanced at Josh. He shrugged in response.

Nick continued. "Between late last night and this morning, I've had five guests complain items are missing from their rooms." He handed a handwritten list to Josh, who looked at it and then handed it to her. "If it had been just one or two items, I could have covered the loss on my own. But the missing items together have a value of over twenty thousand dollars. I'm going to have to report the thefts to our insurance company, which means I'll also have to file a police report."

"Do we have a time frame for the thefts?" Josh asked.

"Two couples left their rooms around five last night. The others not until around seven when the reunion started. The earliest anyone got back to their room was midnight."

"I'll go through the security tapes. See if I can find anyone entering the rooms."

"We have to get this resolved. My investors won't want to sink money into a hotel where the guests are being robbed." He dropped his head into his hands for a minute, pinching the bridge of his nose. Until then, she hadn't noticed the dark circles under Nick's eyes, or the jumbled-up hair, like he'd been running his hands through it, or that he still wore the same suit from yesterday that now sported some serious wrinkles. "Tell me you have a suspect. Tell me we're close to solving this case?"

Josh glanced her way and gave a slight nod. "We have a couple of people we're watching but no solid proof yet," she said. "Last night could actually help. If we can catch them on video, we'll have reason to search their lockers or cabins if they're staying on the property."

"Who are you looking at?"

"Shane Rodgers and Colby Summerton, who work in the stables, as well as Ed and Alice Wilkes."

"Wilkes? They worked here before the thefts started," Nick said.

"They also lied during their interviews. They told me and Mac their hometown was Pittsburgh."

"They grew up here. I knew Ed's parents." Nick ran his hand over his mouth as he shook his head. He'd always said he considered his staff to be like family. Hearing that a family member might have betrayed him, one whose parents were friends of his, had to be a big shock. "I don't know the stable hands. They're new, but I want to see solid proof before we accuse anyone. We need to catch them in the act so there's no way they can deny their involvement."

How were they supposed to do that? Genny knew that Josh had watched hundreds of hours of video already. Were they supposed to stake out each floor? Because if so, they didn't have the manpower.

"Actually, I have an idea how we can accomplish that, sir," Josh said.

Josh laid out his plan. When he got the boss's approval, he excused himself to go make the arrangements.

Genny sat up straighter in her chair. "Sir, should we bring Mac into this? It would give us another set of eyes."

Nick was tapping his fingers on his desk, staring at the wall. At her question, he shifted his gaze to meet her. "No. I know he's your supervisor, but he's been acting weird. Coming and going without notice. His work's been sloppy and late. I think we're going to see some changes around here soon. We just need to get this other situation wrapped up first."

Genny could tell Nick about Mac's job interview, but even as much as she disliked the man, it wasn't her right to share that news. What if Mac didn't get the Orlando job and Nick fired him? Genny didn't want to see anyone lose their job, especially because of her. She kept quiet. Instead, she texted Liz to cancel their mani-pedi date for that afternoon.

Liz texted back. WHAT'S GOING ON? SOMEONE SAID THEY SAW YOU GO INTO NICK'S OFFICE THIS MORNING. TODAY'S YOUR DAY OFF. I'LL EXPLAIN EVERYTHING SOON.

Genny's phone buzzed with a new text, this time from Josh. "Sir, we're all set. Eric and Heather Thomas will arrive at one today."

Nick logged into his computer and reserved their best and most expensive suite. The Rosewood faced the back of the resort, overlooking the pool and in the distance the Chihuahuan Desert. It had a living room, a separate bedroom with a king bed, and a bathroom to die for. The walk-in shower was the size of her entire bathroom. The balcony off the main room held a dining table and a full-sized hot tub where the guests could gaze at the stars as they relaxed.

Together, they left the office and made their first stop at the front desk. Nick motioned for the weekend concierge to join the front-desk staff. "I have some special guests arriving today. They are to be treated as VIPs. Give them anything they ask for, no matter how odd. Understood?" Everyone nodded, then went back to their jobs.

Genny made a quick stop at her office, where she changed out of her jeans, blouse, and sneakers into her blue and white pioneer dress. A few minutes later, Josh knocked on her door. They made a stop at housekeeping to inform Marta of the VIPs' arrival, with instructions that no one was to bother them unless the guests asked for something or the CLEAN ME sign was on the door. From there, they walked to the tour office and let Hank and Alice know they had VIPs arriving and that Mr. and Mrs. Eric Thomas had requested a private "twilight stagecoach ride" for that evening. Genny told Alice to enjoy the evening off. They made similar stops at the arcade and mercantile before stopping at the café, where Liz ushered them to her office in the back.

"What on earth is going on?" she asked.

Genny filled her in on the most recent string of thefts and Josh's plan to flush out the culprits once and for all. Liz promised to let her staff know about the VIPs and offered any help Josh needed from her.

As they walked back out into the midmorning heat, Genny turned to Josh. "What now?"

"How about we grab some grub from the café and you can help me go through last night's video feed?"

At one p.m. sharp, Genny and Josh were back outside the resort's front doors to greet the VIPs. A black stretch limo pulled up to the door. Nick would groan and complain about the extra expense, but once his firm solved this case, he would change his tune. The driver came around and opened the passenger door. Eric Thomas exited the car first in crisp, creased black jeans and a black polo shirt. He held his hand toward the open car door. Heather slipped her hand into his and stepped out. Her left ring finger sported a diamond that deserved its own zip code. She wore a pristine white dress with thin straps and spiked heels that sparkled almost as much as her ring. Diamond drop earrings with a matching teardrop necklace completed the look.

She was...expensive. Out of place. Clueless. And the perfect target.

Genny leaned in close. "Who wears white in the desert?"

"Someone who's careless and wouldn't think twice about leaving her possessions lying around because she thinks she's above everyone else. She doesn't have to lock up her stuff. No one would dare cross her husband. Besides, it's just stuff. Stuff that can be replaced because they've got so much money it doesn't matter."

"Are those stones real?" she whispered.

Josh chuckled. "Real enough."

Heather clung to Eric's arm, a delighted smile brightening her features. "Darling, this place is amazing. Did you see the wooden sidewalk? You could use this place as a movie set."

"I knew you'd love it," Eric said.

"Showtime," Josh whispered.

Genny stepped forward. "Mr. and Mrs. Thomas, welcome to the Prickly Pear Resort. I'm Genevieve Bowen. If there's anything I can do to make your stay more pleasant, please don't hesitate to let me know."

"That's very sweet of you. I believe my husband is chomping at the bit to catch up with his friend, Nick Colangelo. Maybe this big, strong, handsome man can help get our bags to our room? Eric has promised me that you have a pool and a lounger under a cabana for me. After that flight from LA, I just want fresh air and quiet."

"Of course," said Genny. "This is Doc Holliday, and he's at your service. Mr. Thomas, if you'll follow me, I'll take you to Mr. Colangelo. He's waiting for you in his private suite."

"Thank you." Eric gave Heather a quick kiss on the cheek. "Honey, I'll meet you at the pool in a bit."

Eric clapped Josh on the shoulder while passing him a hundred-dollar bill. "Thanks, Doc."

"My pleasure." Josh grabbed the baggage cart and loaded up the half-dozen suitcases from the trunk. This was all part of the plan. While Eric met with Nick, Josh would escort Heather to the room and set up the hidden camera. "Mrs. Thomas, ma'am, if you'll follow me. We'll get you settled and poolside in no time."

As they walked to the elevator, Heather chatted away, making sure that those within range could hear her. "This place is so much fun. It's like stepping back in time. Why, just look at that staircase and the wallpaper. Oh, and you know what my husband did? He arranged for a private stagecoach tour for us tonight so we can watch the sunset over the desert. It's our anniversary."

"Congratulations. How many years?" Josh unobtrusively scanned the room to see if anyone appeared a little too interested in Heather.

"Twenty-five, but it feels like yesterday." She ran her fingertips over her pendant. "This was last year's gift. I can't imagine how Eric can possibly top it, but I have faith that whatever he gives me this year will be simply stunning."

"I'm sure it will be, ma'am."

They had to share the elevator with another couple, and they passed other guests and housekeeping in the hall leading up to the suite. Heather kept her commentary running. Josh responded when needed, but he was busy going through the plan in his head. He'd called the police department that morning and brought them up to speed on what had been happening at the hotel. Josh could expose the culprits, but he needed help from the local PD to make the actual arrests.

Once in the room, Heather and Josh got to work. She went to the bedroom, changed into pool attire, and left her diamond necklace, earrings, and ring on the dresser. After all, she wouldn't want tan lines to mess up her look. Josh hid the first camera aimed at the door. Then he hid a second camera in the bedroom. Genny was in her office watching the feed as she talked to him on his cell. As soon as he was done, he headed to join her. Heather would wait ten minutes and then go to the pool. Besides the room cameras, Heather also wore sunglasses with a hidden camera in case the bandits robbed her en route to or from the pool.

Sitting on Genny's desk were two dome-covered plates. She'd turned her computer around to face the visitor chairs.

"What's all this?" he asked.

She gave a little half shrug and smiled as pink stole over her cheeks. "Stakeouts require food, right? Before Nick's call, I had planned to invite you over to my place for dinner tonight. Since there's a good chance you won't be free then, I decided a working lunch was the next best thing."

Normally, his stakeout food consisted of a bag of chips and a stale convenience store sandwich. Genny had definitely upped the game and the appeal of a good surveillance session.

"Hopefully I'll still be able to take you up on that dinner offer."

They settled in and watched the monitor. Heather left the room. Other guests came and went down the hallway. Housekeeping went in and out of other rooms. Food service delivered lunch to a room across from the suite. But no one even glanced at the Rosewood suite's door.

A text buzzed Josh's phone, followed by another. "Heather and Eric are on their way to get dressed for the stagecoach ride.

Tombstone PD has two plainclothes officers on-site now. They're in the café, but when Heather and Eric come out, they'll make their way toward the main building."

"Josh, relax. I know my part. Stay in my office and watch the room feed. If anyone goes into the suite, call the police. Just be careful out there and try to remember, you're not really Doc Holliday."

Josh picked up his hat and tipped it her way. "Now Miz Genny, don't you worry yourself about me. I'm a trained professional."

"Just end this, Josh. Safely."

He planned to do just that.

CHAPTER THIRTEEN

Genny took a deep breath then blew it out slowly as she counted to ten and said a prayer asking God to keep Josh and everyone else safe. So far, the bandits had never hurt anyone or even come close, but even a tame animal could attack when cornered. To keep her mind from spiraling, she cleaned her desk then ran a cloth across all the flat surfaces in her office, all the while keeping an eye on the video feed. When there was nothing left to clean, she settled into her chair to stare at an empty room.

Minutes ticked by that felt like hours.

Stakeouts without Josh are boring.

How does he do this?

I should have grabbed some chocolate.

Her thoughts swirled around and around but always came back to Josh and what came next. While she found this particular aspect of investigating boring, she could see how the whole thing appealed to him. He was a protector through and through. In school, he'd been the one to sit with the new kid or stand up for the one getting bullied. He was also a helper. He'd volunteer to tutor, he'd put up Christmas lights at the senior center, and he always did the dishes for her mom when he came for dinner. Being a private investigator might not have been Josh's initial goal, but it fit him.

As she'd escorted Eric to Nick's suite, the man had bragged nonstop about Josh and his investigative skills. How highly his colleagues and management throughout the company regarded Josh. Eric said he wouldn't be surprised if his superiors offered Josh a promotion to head up his own office someday soon. Her heart swelled with pride on his behalf.

But it also made her think.

What chance did they have of making it as a couple?

Sure, they could alternate driving to Phoenix or Tombstone on their days off, but then what? Would that really allow them to build a solid foundation for a lifelong relationship? There was nothing in Tombstone for Josh except for her. His family had moved. The town didn't need a private investigator. Nick's need was the exception, not the rule. What would he even investigate here? Phoenix, on the other hand, had plenty to offer Josh. And if she was being truthful, her too.

But she was so close to achieving her goal. For as long as she could remember, she'd been working toward making hotel manager. Okay, she wasn't really close to hitting that milestone. Nick would never retire. She'd have to settle for Human Resources Manager. That was, if Nick even offered her the job. Would that satisfy her?

Movement on the computer screen made her forget all about promotions. The suite door opened. In walked a woman wearing a straw sun hat and a sundress, carrying a large purse. Definitely not Heather. Genny texted the officers to make their move. The woman glanced around while keeping her face covered. *Was she on to them?* She moved into the bedroom. Genny switched her attention to the second camera. The uninvited guest went straight to the dresser and picked up the necklace. She even tried it on, and when she turned to the mirror to see herself, the video caught her face.

There you are.

Genny gave a little fist pump as warmth spread throughout her body, followed by a tightness in her chest. She should have caught the lie. She'd hired a couple of crooks. The loss Nick had experienced sat squarely on her shoulders.

Genny stared at the computer screen, watching, as the thief pocketed the jewelry lying out, then rifled through the drawers. She dropped a few other trinkets and even some clothes into her purse before she opened the suite door to two of Tombstone's finest.

Genny sent a text to Josh.

We got her.

Josh sat on the floor of the stagecoach as his teeth rattled and his head bounced on the coach walls with every bump and dip in the trail. He'd left Genny's office and snuck down to Hank's shed, where he'd climbed into the coach to hide. Eric had almost stepped on him when he'd climbed in after Heather for their private ride.

Alice Wilkes had asked Hank twice if he was sure she wasn't needed. When Hank told her to go enjoy her free time, she'd made a comment about a book she was reading and left. Josh hadn't been surprised, figuring at least one of the ring members would hit the room.

The buzz from his phone caught his attention. As he pulled out his cell, Eric and Heather ignored him, keeping their gaze focused on the horizon.

WE GOT HER.

Josh read the text out loud.

"That was fast," Eric said.

"Darling, only a fool of a thief would have passed on those rocks. They're very good fakes."

Eric nodded toward the window.

"Looks like it's showtime here as well. Got three riders coming at us fast."

Josh texted his contact. Now.

Josh kept scrunched down on the floor. The bandits wouldn't be able to see him unless they poked their heads in through the window.

"Driver, stay where you are," a man called out.

Eric turned so his body blocked the inside of the stagecoach. "What's going on here?"

The man moved his horse closer. The other two disappeared, and Josh guessed they'd moved in front of the coach to keep them from going anywhere. Unknown to the riders, he'd installed a camera on the side of the coach and could now see on his phone app a perfect shot of the Gentleman Bandit. Just like Genny described, he had his hat pulled down and a bandanna over the lower half of his face. But Josh recognized the voice.

"This here's a holdup." The man held out a black cloth bag. "Now, you folks cooperate, and everything will be just fine. Put your wallets, watches, and jewelry in there, and then we'll be on our way."

"What if we don't cooperate?" Eric asked.

"Well, we could take your horses. Leave you out in the desert. You're a couple of miles from the resort. You'd make it there in an hour or so. That is, if the desert animals and reptiles leave you alone."

Heather sucked in a gasp.

The rider shoved the bag closer to Eric. "I'm guessing the little lady isn't up to a walk back to the resort in that fancy dress of hers."

Eric took the bag, and he and Heather went through the motions to buy them time. Heather gave Josh a thumbs-up that let him know she'd spotted vehicles headed their way.

"Boss," one of the other bandits called out, "we got company."

The Gentleman Bandit went to swing around on his saddle, and Eric reached out and grabbed the reins. He quickly tied them around the door frame, trapping the rider from taking off. The bandit pulled on the leather straps, but they held tight. The other two riders took off, leaving him behind. While everyone was watching the Gentleman Bandit's friends, Josh slipped out the opposite door and ran around the coach, catching the big guy as he slid off his horse. Josh grabbed his arm before he could run.

"Hold it right there, *Ed*." He pulled the bandanna down, exposing the man's full face. "Game over, and you lose."

The police caught the two on horseback, cuffed them, and put them in one of the police vehicles. The other officer led the horses to the coach and handed the reins to Hank, who tied all three horses to the rear. He'd return them to the barn. The police cuffed Ed and took him into custody.

"Oh, Ed," Josh called out, "don't worry about Alice. She'll be waiting for you at the police station...in the cell next to yours."

Josh sent one last text before they made the trip home.

CASE CLOSED.

CHAPTER FOURTEEN

Monday morning Genny sat in her office as she'd done so many times before. Except everything had changed in the last couple of weeks. For eleven years she'd called the Prickly Pear Resort her second home. But recent events had cast an ugly shadow on the place. Now, she had a decision to make.

Nick had just left her office. Mac had resigned via email that morning, and Nick had promoted her to human resources manager. He hadn't asked her if she wanted the job. Why would he? It had been her goal for years. But what Nick didn't know was that Genny knew why Ed and Alice Wilkes had targeted the Prickly Pear and Nick in particular. She knew how Nick had forced Ed's parents to sell their property below market. How he'd not only run the Wilkes family off their land but others. The Prickly Pear sat on tainted land, in Genny's opinion.

For years, she'd looked up to Nick.

Not anymore.

Just being in the same room with the man left an oily feeling on her skin.

How could she keep working for him? And what would she do instead?

As her gut churned over her predicament, she prayed for guidance and wisdom. But until she found her answers, she had work to do. Nick had given her a ton of paperwork, including filing insurance claims for the thefts. It didn't fall under the umbrella of human resources, but what else could she do?

Instead of completing the paperwork, however, she stared at the clock. Heather and Eric had checked out and returned to Phoenix yesterday. Josh had a bit of work to finish for Nick before he would follow them.

Just the thought of him leaving sent her back in time. Tears trickled down her cheeks. Oh, she was being silly. Phoenix was a three-hour drive. It wasn't like the man was moving across the country again. And she wasn't a scared teenager anymore.

But seeing him once a week or whenever their schedules aligned wasn't the same. It wasn't what she'd hoped for.

A soft knock had her quickly wiping the moisture from her face. "Come in."

Josh pushed the door open, and her heart soared with delight. He had a cup carrier in one hand and a Sarsaparilla Café bag in the other. "Have time for a lunch break?"

"Only if we can take it outside. The walls are closing in on me today." She took one look at her tablet then left it behind.

It was another glorious day in Tombstone. Blue skies, white fluffy clouds, and temperatures hot enough to fry an egg on the sidewalk. Within minutes, her dress stuck to her back as beads of sweat ran down her spine. And she didn't care about any of that because she had Josh at her side.

They lucked out, and the picnic table under the palm trees was free. Josh handed her a drink—lemon iced tea—before pulling out their food. She wasn't really hungry, especially not with her stomach a jumbled-up mess of nerves. But she'd pretend for his sake.

"The police arrested Shane, Colby, and their roommate this morning. It seems the three of them had plans to open their own resort and have been stealing company information from here and the place in town where the roommate worked."

"So that's why they were sneaking around?"

"Yep. It's also why Ed could get to the horses without being seen. He knew that the two of them were always leaving the barn and nosing around the resort. Oh, I forgot to tell you. They found your necklace. It was still in Ed and Alice's cabin. The police have to keep it for now as evidence, but they promised you'll get it back as soon as possible."

She pressed her palm against her heart as relief flooded through her, but it only lasted for a minute. Unless she figured a few things out, she'd be like her ancestor, Laura Genevieve McDaris, who lost her first love.

"So, you've got everything wrapped up then? Nothing left to do, and you'll be leaving today?"

He unwrapped his burger and, for a moment, she thought he was going to ignore her question. Then his gaze met hers, and she saw a flare of hope.

"Not yet. My boss gave me the rest of the week off. I told him I had unfinished business in town."

"Do you now?"

"Yeah. I haven't had time to stop by and see your parents."

A small thrill streaked through her. "They'd love to see you."

"But that's not all."

"It isn't?"

"No. See, there's this woman who's captured my heart over the last couple of weeks."

"Hmm. I see."

He laid his hand over hers, softly caressing the skin. "Do you?"

"I might be in the same predicament."

"Any suggestions on what I should do?" he asked.

The same question had run around and around in her head all morning. "Well, it depends on what your plans are. What are you asking of her?"

He took both her hands in his. "I'm asking her to give me a chance. To give our love a chance."

"She loves you?"

"I think she does. I know I love her."

Genny bit down on her lip to keep from responding. She needed answers to a few things first.

"You asked what my plans are. Well, I'd like to head up my own office. Right now, based on what my boss said, I'm on track for a promotion to do just that. The lead investigator in San Francisco is retiring next year. My name's been brought up."

Her heart stuttered. "California. Wow. That's amazing…and far."

"It is."

"You'll make a great lead investigator, Josh. They'll be lucky to have you."

He squeezed her hand. "But will you? Would you go to California with me?"

"After just finding each other again and going on two dates?" She sat back, pulling her hands out of his hold. "Josh, that's a big ask."

"Three. I count the stakeout. There was food involved."

She laughed. It was better than crying. "Okay, three dates, and you want me to think about something a year down the road? I don't know, Josh. I've never lived anywhere but here. I just got a promotion today."

"Hey, that's great news. Congratulations." He smiled, but it didn't reach his eyes.

"But I don't think I want to take it."

"Why?"

"Because I don't know if I can work for someone like Nick. He forced those families to sell their property to him. Who knows what other shady deals he's done? And if I want to work in management elsewhere, I still need my bachelor's degree."

She jumped up, too agitated to sit. She paced back and forth. On the third pass, Josh stood in front of her.

"Genny, tell me what you want. But first, answer this. Do you love me?" He cupped her face with his hands. He held her like she was the most precious thing on the planet. "It should be an easy question, love."

"It is, because I do and have since I first saw you. But it wasn't enough last time. What makes this different?"

"We're older, wiser, braver. And I love you too much to just walk away. If my moving to California is a deal breaker, I won't do it."

"I don't even know what the deal is, Josh."

"It's simple. I want us to be together. If I have to give up my job and move to Tombstone, I will. If I have to pass on a move, I will. I'll do whatever it takes. Because you're worth it, Genny. You are my everything."

"I can't ask you to give up your job and especially not move back here. I've been thinking. What if I found a job in Phoenix and went to college at the same time? I'd have to figure out housing—"

"You could stay with my sister. She told me this weekend her roommate is moving out, and she loves you."

Genny considered this. "Okay, if she says yes, that's one obstacle. I'd have to find a job."

"You know Nick would write you a glowing recommendation."

"I hope so. Josh, I'm willing to move to Phoenix, but not if it means we'll have to up and move again in a year. I want a family of my own someday. I want children who will know their grandparents and cousins. I want big, loud holidays, and I want to plant roots. I want a home that I can measure my children's growth and run my fingers over those marks when they've grown and moved. But I also want you to be happy. I'm not asking for all of these things right now. We have time, but only if it's what we both want."

"Genny, it's everything I want, but only if you're by my side. I might have to wait a little longer to be my own boss in Phoenix, but it'll be worth it if I have you with me." He dropped to his knee and pulled a small box out of his pocket. He opened it to reveal a ring with a purple rose that had a diamond in the center. She didn't have to look to know that "Josh and Genny Forever" was engraved on the inside of the band.

"My ring. You kept it."

"Genny, I gave you this promise years ago, and it's the same now. With this ring, I promise to love you until my last breath. I promise to stand by your side and give you whatever you need. I promise to always be your best friend. I promise that when you're ready, I will ask you to be my wife. Until then, this ring will remind you of my love and that I'll always be here for you." He slipped the ring on her left hand. "What do you say?"

She looked down at the ring on her finger, remembering the last time he'd placed it there and when she'd returned it. This time she'd do it differently. This time, she'd be brave and honor her promise to him.

"I say yes to Phoenix and you and us. I promise to love you for always, Joshua Mendoza, and the next time I take this ring off, it will be because you put another one in its place."

When Josh stood, he took her in his arms and kissed her. In that moment, their future looked as bright as the blazing Arizona sun.

Dear Reader,

Thank you for spending your time with our stories. We had so much fun writing *Love's a Mystery in Hazardville, Connecticut,* that we jumped at the chance to team up again. Tombstone is a place almost all of us have heard about, and we thought it'd be fun to explore the town, the people, and their stories a little deeper.

While we both currently call Connecticut home, we originally come from different parts of the country. Writing brought Bethany and me together. We joined a local writers' group way back when we were just starting out, and from there our friendship bloomed. Over the years, we've bounced ideas off of each other, problem-solved, and laughed a lot.

We sincerely hope you enjoy our stories of love, letting go of the past, and connecting.

Sincerely,
Gail and Bethany

About the Authors

Bethany John

Bethany John is a writer and schoolteacher who currently resides in an idyllic small town in western Connecticut. In her free time, she enjoys spending time at the lake and hanging out with her large extended family.

Gail Kirkpatrick

Gail Kirkpatrick is the pen name for a multi-published romantic mystery, contemporary romance, and women's fiction author. Gail learned to read at her grandpa's knee at the age of three. Since then, she's devoured books in all genres. She loves to bake, watch funny animal videos, and watch the sunset over the Long Island Sound. As a former Navy wife, she's lived in eight states and three countries and brings that knowledge to her stories. These days she calls Connecticut home along with her amazing husband, kids, and a demanding pup.

Story Behind the Name

~⊙ ⊙~

Tombstone, Arizona

In early 1877, US Army scout Ed Schieffelin was stationed at Camp Huachuca about fifteen miles north of the US-Mexico border. Part of his job was to go on missions to find valuable ore samples. When fellow scout and friend, Al Sieber, heard what Ed Schieffelin was doing, it is rumored that he said, "The only rock you will find out there will be your own tombstone." Another story quotes Sieber as saying, "Better take your coffin with you, Ed. You will only find your tombstone there, and nothing else."

Either way, Sieber was wrong. After months of working and searching, Ed Schieffelin did find something of value. In the hills east of the San Pedro River, Ed found pieces of silver ore on a high plateau called Goose Flats. Many more months of searching led him to the source, a vein fifty feet long and twelve inches wide. At that time, Schieffelin took on a partner, William Griffith, to finance the mining of the ore. Griffith is the one who filed the original claim, which was named Tombstone.

Jalapeno Cheddar Cornbread

Ingredients:

3 cups all-purpose flour

1 cup yellow cornmeal

¼ cup sugar

2 tablespoons baking powder

2 teaspoons salt

2 cups milk

3 extra-large eggs, lightly beaten

½ pound (2 sticks) unsalted butter, melted, plus extra to grease the pan

1/3 cup green onions, chopped, plus extra for garnish

3 tablespoons seeded and minced fresh jalapeño peppers

4 ounces aged extra-sharp cheddar cheese, grated and divided

4 ounces Monterey Jack cheese, grated and divided

Directions:

1. Preheat oven to 350 degrees.

2. Combine flour, cornmeal, sugar, baking powder, and salt in large bowl. In separate bowl, combine milk, eggs, and butter. Stir wet ingredients into dry until most of the lumps are dissolved. Stir in green onions, jalapeños, and all but ¼ cup of each cheese. Allow mixture to sit at room temperature for up to 30 minutes.

3. Grease 9x13-inch pan.

4. Pour batter into prepared pan, smooth the top, and sprinkle with remaining grated cheese and green onions.

5. Bake for 30 to 35 minutes or until toothpick comes out clean.

6. Cool and cut into large squares. Serve warm with butter. Add drizzle of honey for extra kick!

*Read on for a sneak peek of another exciting book
in the Love's a Mystery series!*

Love's a Mystery *in*
Peculiar, Missouri
by Emily Quinn & Laura Bradford

Love Is Growing
By Emily Quinn

Baltimore, Maryland

1960

Rhoda Grey studied herself in the mirror. The new bright orange and green dress she'd bought over the weekend felt too short for work. Or maybe her legs were just too long. Either way, the outfit wasn't modest enough for her job at the insurance office. She sat on the bed and checked the length again. No matter what the salesgirl had told her, there was no way she could pull this off. She wanted to look more like the women she watched on television. Like Mrs. Kennedy as she campaigned for her husband. The only problem was Rhoda hated hats and couldn't afford designer clothes. She'd gone with something the salesclerk had assured her everyone was wearing. She carefully took the dress off and put it back on the hanger. She'd have to take it back after work. Although she didn't know what she'd buy to replace it. All the dresses seemed to be more in tune with being a fun, young chick going to a concert rather than the office. She was definitely not a chick. No matter what the vernacular of the day wanted to call her.

She hurried and dressed in her standard Monday outfit and didn't look in the mirror. She knew how she looked. Drab, old, and grey, just like her name. No wonder she was getting passed over for promotion. No one could see her. Although how she was overlooked when she towered over every other woman on her floor she didn't know.

Rhoda grabbed her coat and her purse. Before heading to work, she wanted to run upstairs to the rooftop and check on her tomato plants. The warm weather and mild temperature for the last few days had helped the seedlings, but she still worried about a frost in these early first days of May. She'd grown the plants from seed and they were still tiny. Their size was an advantage if it did freeze. It kept them close to the ground and out of the worst of the night air. Still, maybe she had a few minutes before she needed to catch her bus.

She quickly locked her door and took the stairs to the rooftop. Her apartment was on the fifth floor so it didn't take long. The five pots were exactly where she'd left them yesterday. Lined up by the edge of the rooftop, sheltered by a brick wall that would heat up in the sunshine and give the plants warmth long after the sun had set. She touched one leaf, her thoughts going to her childhood home where she'd helped her mother plant the garden every spring.

Now that house was gone, having been sold to pay for the funeral costs after the accident that killed her parents. She was alone in this world and because of that, she needed to get to work. The only person she could count on was herself.

She could see the moon, slipping out of view as the sun rose. Presidential candidates were talking about sending a man to the moon. It looked like a long, lonely trip. She liked being on the ground. Even being up on the rooftop, although necessary for the plants to get consistent sunlight to grow, was too high for Rhoda. She felt connected to the earth, or she had when she'd gardened with her mother. The memory was so long ago now, her grasp on it was fleeting. Or was if she was doing anything besides working with her plants. She said a quick goodbye to the plants and hurried downstairs.

Riding the bus to work, she watched as they drove through different neighborhoods, gathering people from all walks of life. Caucasian, Hispanic, African American, a person's background didn't matter on the bus. It was truly the melting pot she'd learned about in school. Everyone just waited to start their workday. Some people chatted about their families and events they were going to, but she didn't have anyone to talk with. She nodded to the woman who'd sat down next to her. "Good morning, happy Monday."

The woman grunted and then leaned back and closed her eyes.

Not interested in conversation, then. Rhoda turned to the window and to watching the world go by outside the bus. She always tried, but she never seemed to find someone willing to share their thoughts with her, not even for a few minutes stuck in the same vehicle.

Instead, she planned out her next row of plants. The building manager didn't mind her using the rooftop for her plants as long as she took care of them and didn't just let them die and look bad. Clarence was very concerned about the way the public areas of the building looked, which she appreciated. It was nice coming home to a clean entryway. A lot of the buildings around her didn't look as friendly or inviting. Maybe later this summer she'd ask if she could plant flowers on the outside step. There were two empty planter boxes that Clarence never filled with life. Daisy's would be nice against the red brick. Or purple petunias.

She realized that her stop was next and she stood as they approached the corner. The driver glanced back and caught her movement, calling out the street corner. The woman who'd been sitting next to her was already gone. She'd must have left during Rhoda's musing about flowers.

The city was preparing for the Democratic rally that was being held that weekend. Street sweepers were cleaning the debris from the streets, and landscapers hung baskets on the streetlights. The town looked pretty, like what she imagined a small town might look like. Adding the plants to the concrete and steel made it feel more approachable. She might stay around to maybe catch a glimpse of the congressman who was now running for president. The news said he was drop-dead gorgeous. Of course, that one factor wasn't enough to win Rhoda's vote in November.

The noise of the city hit her as soon as she stepped off the bus and onto the sidewalk. Horns honked, vehicles drove past, and the doors on the bus slammed shut behind her as it took off for its next stop. She weaved through people on the walkway and finally reached the doors to her office building. When she stepped inside the foyer, the line to the elevator almost reached the door. Instead of waiting there, she clocked in at the timeclock and then headed to the stairs to start her day.

At her desk, she tucked her purse into her drawer, hung up her coat on a hook in her cubical, then opened the first file in her inbox. She had two boxes. One was labeled in, the other out. Her supervisor, April, came in earlier than the clerks. Then, she walked around the floor and dropped off the day's work on each desk. At random times during the day, she'd come back and take away the files in the out box. Rhoda always had more in her inbox at the beginning of the day than the other clerks. Yet, when the supervisor slot had opened, she hadn't even been interviewed for the position. She'd gotten a form letter thanking her for her interest, but a more qualified candidate had been chosen.

She knew that April, who'd gotten the position, had never been the top producer, but she did have one skill Rhoda didn't. She talked a lot. And to everyone. Rhoda couldn't even imagine chatting with everyone on the floor including the bosses as they came by. How would she get any work done?

At ten, April came to her desk and picked up the completed files. "You've done a lot of work this morning. I'm so lucky to have you in my group. Mr. Henry would like you to come to his office for a minute, please." April held her arm out like Rhoda didn't know where Mr. Henry's office was located.

Rhoda stood and ran her hands down the cotton dress she'd put on that morning. Now, she was glad she hadn't taken the chance on the orange one, but she'd wished she had something newer on. She pushed her hair back off her shoulders. "Do you know what he wants to talk about?"

April shook her head. "I tried to ask, but he said it was personal and I was to go get you. If they ask if I'm doing a good job, please say yes. I really need this position."

For a minute, Rhoda really saw the woman behind the mask April put on every day. She was just as nervous about this as Rhoda was, especially if it was an evaluation of the new supervisor's abilities. She smiled at April. "You're doing a great job."

The woman blinked and then smiled back. "Thank you. I thought, well, I assumed you would be the one they promoted. You're so good at all this."

Yes, I'd thought that as well. Rhoda hoped the opinion didn't show on her face. "Thank you for saying that. I better get going and see what Mr. Henry wants."

"Oh yes, of course." April stepped back, letting Rhoda step out of her cube toward the line of offices by the windows.

She knocked on Mr. Henry's door and stepped inside when she heard his response.

"Miss Grey, I'd like to introduce you to Mr. Reynolds. He's our corporate attorney and would like to speak with you." Mr. Henry made the introduction to the man standing next to him, then to Rhoda's surprise, Mr. Henry stepped out of the office. He paused at the door. "Take as long as you need. I'll be getting some coffee."

Mr. Reynolds pointed to the visitor chair, then moved to sit behind Mr. Henry's desk. "This won't take long. I've received correspondence from an attorney in Missouri. Apparently, this Jacob Stine didn't have your home address, so his office reached out here asking if I'd play intermediary with this."

Rhoda hurried and sat in the chair she'd been directed to. "I'm sorry, Mr. Reynolds, what exactly are you handling?"

"You've apparently been named as a beneficiary in a will. A Mr. Fredrick James left you a farm and some belongings in a small town in Missouri. It's near the Kansas border. I'm sure it's not much, but it is yours." He passed her a copy of the will as he studied her. "Here's the documents. I'm sure Mr. Henry would approve some leave for you to go there and settle the estate. You may come back with some money to buy a new dress or two."

"I looked for a new dress this weekend, it's just hard…" Rhoda stopped talking. Mr. Reynolds wasn't really interested in her clothes. "Anyway, I don't understand. I inherited a farm?"

"Just what a young career girl in Baltimore needs, right?" He stood and held out his hand. "Congratulations. There's a list of people you need to contact. If you don't want to go across the country to settle this, I've been told that there are several offers to purchase the land. You could just do most of it from here. They'll explain all that when you call."

"Thank you for letting me know." She shook his hand and clutched at the envelope he'd given her with the other.

"Just keep Mr. Henry informed about what your plan is. I hear you're a valuable part of his team." The look he gave her as he walked out of the office showed he didn't believe that anyone who looked like her could be a valuable part of any team.

She sank back into the chair and read the will. When she finished, she leaned back, shocked. What was she going to do with a farm in Missouri? In a town named, Peculiar, no less.

A Note from the Editors

~⚬ ⚬~

We hope you enjoyed another volume in the Love's a Mystery series, created by Guideposts. For over seventy-five years, Guideposts, a nonprofit organization, has been driven by a vision of a world filled with hope. We aspire to be the voice of a trusted friend, a friend who makes you feel more hopeful and connected.

By making a purchase from Guideposts, you join our community in touching millions of lives, inspiring them to believe that all things are possible through faith, hope, and prayer. Your continued support allows us to provide uplifting resources to those in need. Whether through our communities, websites, apps, or publications, we inspire our audiences, bring them together, and comfort, uplift, entertain, and guide them. Visit us at guideposts.org to learn more.

We would love to hear from you. Write us at Guideposts, P.O. Box 5815, Harlan, Iowa 51593 or call us at (800) 932-2145. Did you love *Love's a Mystery in Tombstone, Arizona*? Leave a review for this product on guideposts.org/shop. Your feedback helps others in our community find relevant products.

Find inspiration, find faith, find Guideposts.
Shop our best sellers and favorites at
guideposts.org/shop
Or scan the QR code to go directly to our Shop

Printed in the United States
by Baker & Taylor Publisher Services